Bad
People

Bad People is the story of Lucy and James as they struggle to earn a living in music.

Their histories and destinies are strangely linked in this world and the next.

The story is linked by 32 original songs.

The novel is complete. The songs are complete.

The songs are not yet voiced correctly. If it was a musical they would be sung by the appropriate characters. For now, they are just 'demos'. However, the demos are live and linkable. If you read this on a PC or Tablet you can click the song links to hear them. If you want a link to all the songs in the order they appear in the novel, then here it is:

https://badpeoplethemusical.bandcamp.com/album/bad-people-the-songs

Hope you like the story and the songs.

Hope you like 'Skulk Rock'.

KOFR

'This is about the continual struggle between good and evil.
The battles rage within us all.'

Bad People

MAX MORPHEUS

Published by Robert T. Morrow

ISBN 978 1 72020178 6 paperback

First published 2018

This edition published 2018

Original music: Robert T. Morrow, Andrew Cutts
© A NeckenderMusic 2014–2018

Main Characters

Lucy Smith
James 'Jimmy English' Smith
Felicia

The Lowdown Dirtkickers

Thunderman – Bass
Mike Remo – Singer/Harp/Sax
The MetroGnome – Drums

The Snakes

Seth Snake – Dead partner of Lucy Smith, Multiple Musical Instruments
Jake 'King' Snake – Guitar, Harmonica, Vocals
Edward 'Sly' Snake – Drums
Simon 'Si' Snake – Guitar
'AJ' Snake – Bass Guitar
Mrs Snake – Wife of Jake

Other Characters

Ronee – Lucy's San Francisco Flatmate
Marv – Marv's Mechanics, Keeps America Rolling
Don Estrada – Leader – Oakland Angels
Al – Trainee Hell's Angel
The Oakland Angels – Musical Hell's Angels
Howard and Elizabeth – Luthier and Wife
English Bob – Saxophone Player from Lincoln City
Wangly Dangly, Adrian The Alien and Boris The Cranium –
    English Bob's friends
Dr Charlie – The Doctor, The Rock and Roll Doctor
Ho Chi Minimum – Bar manager of a Music Bar in Chinatown
Amanda, Yolande and Miranda – Felicia's friends
Rich Guy – Felicia's Fiancee
Dierdre – World's best barmaid
Traffic Cop – Way Cool Female Traffic Cop
Mrs Smith – James' Mum
Mrs Smith (Indistinct Voice) – Lucy's Mum

And

Mr Smith – Starkeeper

Time is upon me like a pack of wolves
Gravity like an avalanche
I got sins I can't absolve
Just like everyone

The cinema in the back of my mind
Keeps replayings all of my crimes
The memories malinger
Like death's cold finger

Distant Meteors, 2009

Contents

Moonlight Over Montana

Lucy Smith loved the line of poplar trees along the top of the hill overlooking the farm. Montana was vast. Vast and lonely and she had started to feel it like never before. She came from suburban Illinois and was beginning to revise her notions of the country life. It was turning out that the infinity of her location of the last 2 years was too much. 'Infinity is too much'; she mused with the phrase and wondered if it could be the start of a song? Sometimes it happened like that; one phrase hooks you in. Not a 'hook line' as such but a 'hook thought' from which other lines would hang in some way. Other times she felt that a ghost visits you and gives you the song. It just appears in your mind and then on the paper in front of you? However it works, there it is; a song! Then, there it was; a song! One of her favourite feelings. Offset by all the failed pages of drivel in her notepad, it is always so worth it when a song is born.

Lucy was a fighter. She figured you don't get gold without panning for it and she wasn't going to give up easily. This being so, she had found herself walking up this hill more and more often to offset the loneliness that had crept into her life here. Since things had soured a little with Seth, she had even begun to welcome the loneliness but somehow these noble trees also provided quiet company and protection for her. She wondered who had planted them and when and even why? The farm had seen better days and Seth and she had not exactly moved it along. So many plans and so much disappointment; ambition is a form of greed. She strummed some chords on her faithful old Gibson 'Nick Lucas' guitar and the music seemed strangely in key with the sound of the breeze in the trees. The farmstead from up here looked like a painting. She often thought of it like that and how the painting could change during the day and evenings. If she was a painter she would be like JMW Turner, the greatest of them all; you would surely need all his skill and vision to capture the Montana skies and sierras on a canvas. It would have to be a big canvas, that's for sure. Vagueness was where it's at now. Life had become vague since her relationship with Seth had declined. She needed to end things and move on but couldn't find a way.

The farm sits neatly in a green valley with distant hills over which the moon often displayed its magnificence. Was it some kind of optical effect in the Montana atmosphere that magnified the moon? Or, was it getting closer, its orbit diminishing? She sometimes could swear she could see highways and houses on there. Whatever; it seemed so close. 'Montana moon show me the way home – I never wanted to be so all alone.' She mentally kicked herself for coming up with formulaic lines like that. It didn't alter the fact that maybe there was a weird gravitational kink over Montana. She would ask her Dad, he had a qualification in Physics. Whatever, it was at that point she decided to leave.

Her mood was lifted as she walked back down the hill. It always was when she knew she'd found a new song. She'd hit on some gorgeous chord sequences and melody to fit and a good start of lyrics. There's a threshold you cross when you know the song will appear and it always lifted her mood. She sang the words to herself as she crossed the farmyard now. She kept her mind on the song not wanting the problems of how to leave Seth take over her mind any more. Had love turned to hate? So many songs out there and she was stuck out here. A shiver ran through her as she thought of how she could tell him. Seth Snake had been the acceptable face of The Snake family dynasty; it hadn't turned out that way. Love hadn't turned to hate yet, but it might, and now was the time to depart. She would tell him tonight when he returned from the gig.

*

Strange how she remembered those thoughts so clearly now, as she now stands back with the faithful poplar trees. Now they silently sway in a light breeze. This time the sky is moonlit but stars, many stars, are also visible. There is a distant mountain range. Again, she looks out over the lower land looking at the farmhouse in the middle distance. She looks down at her hands and the neck of her faithful old Nick Lucas which she now holds with trembling fingers. Splinters of wood dangle where the body was, other fragments dangle from the tangle of strings. She turns a tuning peg and runs a finger over the headstock. She thinks of her father and her 12th birthday when he gave it to her. More tears run down the already marked tracks on her cheek. She takes a deep breath and replays the events between the now and her previous time here earlier today.

Her gaze gradually, and reluctantly, moves down from the guitar remnants and slowly along the intervening meadow to the farmhouse. As her focus tightens she suddenly sees a fire flicker inside one of the windows. Her knuckles whiten even more; one hand gripping the guitar neck, the other in a tight clench by her side. As the flames become visible through the glass her mind's camera moves inside. It sees the cooker ablaze and the whole kitchen begin to catch. She gazes upon the lifeless body of Seth, now grey skinned and slumped. A single bullet wound to the chest and, as the camera moves upwards another bullet hole in the head. Suddenly, flames follow a liquid path from the kitchen to his body and it takes light, doused in the flammable liquid.

Lucy's mind camera slowly backs out of the building and gradually moves the viewpoint back to the raised ground and poplar trees from where she still stares. She jumps back as flames suddenly blow out the windows and engulf the house. So vivid against the surrounding stillness of the night time. She moves forward again and watches impassively as the fire caresses the buildings until a gas cylinder flares high into the night sky.

*

Now her memory cuts back in with flashbacks as if she's watching fragments of a movie that need splicing together. She sees Seth returning home late from his gig and lurching into the room where she was singing her new song. She even remembers thinking to herself that maybe this wouldn't be a good time to tell him she was leaving. She winces as she recalls his reaction to the song. The drunken sneer as he grabs her guitar. The awful sound tsunami as he smashes it against the sideboard. She sees her own face watching impassively other than her tears forming and silently running down her cheeks for the first time that evening.

She sees herself stood as he slumps down onto the couch. She sees herself walk silently from the room as he fumbles with a whisky bottle. He takes a drink and lays his head back. She sees herself open the drawer in the kitchen where he keeps a very large handgun and then walking slowly back into the room. She remembers how it had taken two hands to hold the gun. As he looks up she sees herself shoot him in the chest. His face shows disbelief. She then shoots him in the head. Time stands still except for the expanding cloud of blue smoke from the gunshots. There are two Lucy's in the room; one watching the other in disbelief unable to stop her counterpart. She then sees herself pause for a dilated moment before taking the half drunk bottle from his grasp and, in a vexed act, pouring the remaining whisky over him and then in a trail back to the kitchen. The bottle empties and she throws it to one side in disgust. In some sort of defiance and determination to finish the job she sees herself return with a can of paraffin. She overlays the trail of whisky right into the kitchen to the cooker.

Next, she packs a bag with clothes, boots, a sheaf of manuscripts. Appearing to lose patience with packing, she goes to a drawer and takes out some keys. She walks out to an inconsequential looking farm building. Opening several locks to the door there is an older but well kept Dodge pickup truck. The letters on the front of the bonnet are missing a 'd' and 'e' so that it's a 'Do_g.' She drives 'The Dog' to the front of the farmhouse and walks back in. Several more trips as she throws belongings into the rear tool trunk. On the last trip she loads a saucepan with cooking oil and walks slowly out leaving the gas ring heating the oil on full. Finally, she remembers driving up to the old poplars the long way around as her mind jolts back into the present and she watches the whole farmhouse erupt into flames.

Santa Monica

https://badpeoplethemusical.bandcamp.com/track/santa-monica

And so I stand once again beneath the poplars
Thinking of life without you
Some of us are saved and some of us damned
I remember the touch of your violent hands
Talking to myself no-one heard me

These long shadows disturb me
Life is suddenly lonely
But better than with you around me
And I'm leaving so you can't haunt me

One bullet for your cold heart
One bullet for your evil mind
Who knows what I will find?
I got a brand new start
One last look in your black eyes
The last time in this life
There's no teardrops – as I say goodbye

You made your big mistake
When you found out how much I could take
And now you speak like silence
You were my ideal of violence
Say goodbye to the stars above me
Is there anyone to judge me?
Surrounded by nature's beauty
I bury something so ugly

One bullet for your cold heart
One bullet for your evil mind
Who knows what I will find?
I got a brand new start
One last look in your black eyes
The last time in this life
There's no teardrops – as I say goodbye

Even God won't understand yer
He'll send you back as a black mamba
But you will be in Africa
By the time I'm in Santa Monica

Lucy shivers as the buildings now smoulder in the dawn light. Still she watches. The film running in her mind finally merges with the present and she seems to wake up and shake herself back into reality. As black smokes now rise higher into the still dawn air she walks back and puts her guitar remnants on the passenger seat of

The Dog. As she starts the engine she is startled by a vision of the moon which seems closer than ever through the windscreen of The Dog. She freezes, as if the moon bears witness to her soul. She fights for control of her emotions. She wins and drives off, away from the rising sun and swinging away from the moon. 'Use your last heartbeat chasing your first dream' she sings to herself.

*

Lucy plays songs in her mind as miles and road signs pass. The sun rises over mountains to her left. The road is deserted. Eventually she pulls into a deserted diner and sits in a secluded corner. The waitress seems to smile sympathetically as she takes Lucy's order. Lucy notices finger shaped bruises on her pale slim arms. After her meal and coffee refill she finds the phone booth, shuts the door tightly and dials her mother's number.

'Hi Mom.'

She waits whilst her mother rambles. Eventually,

'You won't be hearing from me for a while.'

Mrs Smith rambles more. Lucy becomes impatient and interrupts,

'YES Mom, I'm ok, but I ended things with Seth.'

There's a pause.

'I thought you might be pleased?'

'No Mom, I'll be ok, I have a plan.'

'I'm going to go to California.'

'I have a truck.'

'It was his but he never ever used it.'

'No Mom, he doesn't mind.'

'No, I don't think we'll hear much from him from here on in.'

'No-one will miss me in Montana Mom, to be honest no-one really knew I was there.'

'Was 2 years solitary.'

'Yes, I love you too Mom.'

'Mom, this is important though, I don't want Seth's family to know where I went so if ANYONE contacts you, you never heard from me in 2 years?.'

'You did teach me to lie Mom?'

'We're bad people aren't we Mom?'

'Tell Dad I love him.'

She sends a kiss down the phone line and hangs up. She looks wide-eyed through the glass of the booth as if in a trance. Her gaze out and along the road. Across a valley there are distant mountains. The future, whatever it holds, is beyond those mountains and under that distant sky. The way things are it might not hold very much at all but she is not about to wait to find out. She needs distance. Distance between her and the Montana moon. Escape velocity from its gravitational pull. It had seen everything.

As she climbs into the truck she pats her guitar remnants on the adjacent seat and pulls away.

Highway

https://badpeoplethemusical.bandcamp.com/track/highway

Use your last heartbeat chasing your first dream
Don't let it go it won't chase you
What did they do to the world you knew?
Time's a thief that much is true
Dream guitars that cry and sing
Dream movie stars in high heels
Dream visions that life can bring
Time's a thief and dreams are what it steals

Scatter me on a highway
Let the trucks take me away
But turn around and I will be there
In your dream or in your nightmare

Second glances in a rear view mirror
Missed chances of history
Circumstances can change your character
No defences to time's robbery

Scatter me on an ocean green
Dark and deep like my sleep
I'll never sleep with the fishes
This life is sweet and delicious

You've come so far – it's come to this
Teardrops running like piss

Life's a long and lonely highway
These dreams were your headlights
Just a ghost drawn by starlight
Driving into the night

Scatter me on a highway
Let the trucks take me away
But turn around and I will be there
In your dream or in your nightmare

Use your last heartbeat chasing your first dream
Don't let it go it won't chase you
Take your last step onto a dance floor
'Cos this is life give me more

Lucy Smith stares ahead as she negotiates the bump and rise of America. She thinks of her youth and the excitement when her father gave her the guitar that his father had given him. She remembers her first song. She remembers her first song notebook. She remembers singing her early songs to Seth. She remembers him smiling and laughing. She remembers his guitar embellishments. She remembers his smile and how sweet their voices sounded together. She remembers her excitement at the notion of building up a life on the farm with him. The highway line hypnotises her. It leads her and keeps her sane.

Still she drives as evening falls. She stares ahead. The highway is quiet. She likes it that way. Her nervousness increases with approaching cars and diminishes as they pass. Vehicles in her rear view mirror make her more nervous though. Much more nervous. She tunes into the sounds of The Dog. She dreads the tone and groove of The Dog changing or, even worse, any unevenness, which may be a sign of impending mechanical failure. As night falls her mind floats upwards up to stars above. They hover and sparkle over mountains in the distance. She gradually accelerates the truck as the dawn chases her. She doesn't notice an eagle high in the sky as the first shafts of sunlight catch its wingspan as it glides over the truck below.

In dawn light she tries to remember how many road junctions she has passed. A compass is stuck to The Dog's dashboard and whenever she is undecided she favours west or south. She figures that each junction makes it more difficult for anyone to follow her tracks. She longs for the state line. She wonders how many state lines will be required to escape 'The Snakes'? She tries to think how many states are between her and the ocean. 'C'mon Dog we're gonna go see the ocean.'

2

She's Too Much

A young teenager sits in his room, somewhere in a cold grey industrial England. He strums a guitar and scribbles in a notebook. As he gazes vacantly through a frosted window his mother enters. She sits quietly staring at him before reaching out and touching his hand tenderly.

'Highly unlikely you'll ever earn a living playing that thing James!'

'No Mum, let's be positive.'

She smiles at his enthusiasm. She always did. Ever since he opened his eyes he had seemed enthusiastic about whatever gained his attentions. The downside was, he was never interested in anything that didn't. As a toddler he never seemed to integrate with mainstream kids and now, at school, he would neglect his studies for the things that fired his imagination. Mostly the guitar!

'Mr Meadows – your illustrious music teacher at school would agree with me?'

'We call him "Flushing" Mum, you know why that is?'

'Of course – Flushing Meadows? Where the tennis tournament is played?'

'No Mum – because he is so full of shit he needs a good flushing.'

Pause

'James!'

They look at each other and then giggle.

The giggle subsides to silence and a sadness takes over.

'You shouldn't have missed the exam James?'

'I don't understand Biology Mum. There's more to life than ameobas.'

'Yes, but you have to start somewhere?'

'If you start at all maybe? Mr Meadows has an amoeba for a brain Mum!'

She giggles, 'That's as maybe. Your father will not be pleased.'

'He wants me to be an accountant. What good is biology for that shit?'

'James!', she sounds a little more severe this time.

Another silence.

She continues, 'Let's just hope he's had a good day at work? You know he just wants you to get to university.'

'Another 3 years of not doing what I want Mum.'

'And what do you want?'

'I want to go to west coast USA and rock Mum.'

'Yes James! And I want to open my back door to a nice country garden with flowers in bloom and an apple tree! We can't have everything we want?'

'Use your last heartbeat chasing your first dream Mum!'

Her face softens and she smiles at him.

'I said I'd go to town tonight with Pete Royle?', as if to ask permission.

Mrs Smith just stares at him smiling knowingly.

'I bet you're going to that pub where the music bands play?'

'Well yes. The Duke of York.'

'And where the girls go?'

He looks at her smiling.

'Ohhhhhh', she smiles back, 'Off you go. I'll deal with your father. Fridays are not usually a bad day for him.'

*

A bright summer morning arrives now and James watches a strange circle of light from his bed. The globe of light tracks across his bedroom ceiling and down the wall. He thinks of it as the moon and its orbit and physics lessons at school. He thinks how strange it is that he like Physics 'cos I fucking hate fucking biology!' He laughs inwardly and tries to work out where the moon will end as it moves on an orbit along and down his wall. And that was when he noticed his guitar wasn't in its usual place. He sits upright in bed and looks around the room. He suddenly stops mentally nursing his hangover as the guitar's absence begins to dominate his mind. He dresses quickly and moves carefully downstairs. His father sits quietly at the breakfast table. His mother is in the small scullery washing dishes. James speaks to her in a low voice

'OK Mum?'

His mother slowly turns her head, looks at him and tries to smile. He sees snail trail tear tracks down her cheeks and moist eyes. Jigsaw thoughts begin to come together.

'It turns out Friday wasn't a good day at all James and your father has to go to work this morning to catch up on things.'

There's a pause.

'Where is it Mum?'

Her tears run now.

'It's in the bin outside.'

James walks out into the backyard and immediately sees the headstock of his old acoustic guitar protruding from the dustbin. The dustbin lid resting precariously on it. As he pulls the neck from the bin a tangle of strings and a broken body follow it. A strange blood circulates in him. His hangover evaporates; his brain crystal clear in its thought schemes. He walks back in and stares at his father and speaks calmly in a fake American accent that cannot disguise his own Manchester accent

'That's my Gibson Nick Lucas man!'

His father stares straight ahead.

'I was going electric anyway. You superfluous old cunt.'

James walks out and doesn't see the tear running down his father's cheek.

*

Now. An older James stands on stage and waits for a count in from a drummer who glances at him and smiles. An American flag with a small sewn on union jack in the top left hangs raggedly at the back of the stage. The singer addresses the audience,

'We're The Lowdown Dirtkickers and you have been our audience.'

An older audience member with a cantilever belly above an ornate belt to his Levis and an oil stained Caterpillar cap manifests a strange walk across the dance area as a show of appreciation. Mike Remo smiles as he continues:

'This is our first time in Susanville and we are definitely going to relocate to this locality. I still wanna meet Susan!'

Female voices around the room shout in excited union,

'I'm Susan!'

Mike Remo laughs as he continues

'On the drums we have THE MetroGnome!'

The Gnome plays a strange Captain Beefheartesque drum lick and smiles at James.

'THE Thunder from way down under is from El Thundero! The Thunderman.'

Thunderman drags the lowest notes you ever heard from his longscale flatwounds and grows the Gnome's lick into a truly weird auditory adventure.

'I'm Mike Reeeeeeemo! The man the girls all wanna know!'

'We're gonna finish with a song by our tame limey on guitar.'

He looks across at James and extends an arm and a smile

'Mr Jimmy English!!!!!!'

The Gnome crescendos and stops as Thunderman lets a long low note hang as it seeks out every corner of the room – 4 clicks and …

Fall

https://badpeoplethemusical.bandcamp.com/track/fall

I put my head out of an aeroplane window
I saw the face of god in his Heaven
Nowhere to be and nowhere to go
A single dice can't roll a 7

All I could do was fall fall fall fall

We'll be hitting the drop zone soon
And I don't want to take you down too
The moment has passed and time turned sour
Life could be over in half an hour

All I can do is fall fall fall fall

So now I only travel in dreams at night
I navigate by city lights
It's a little tricky with an ocean to cross
But I follow boats like an albatross

All I can do is fall fall fall fall

How did I ever get so high?
How did I learn to fly?
I float like an electric ghost
The stars are getting close
Small talk in the small hours of small time in a small town in a small
world
I'm living in a small mind
The drink makes you sad – eventually
And I wish I knew more about good and less about bad
All the angels talk in whispers
And God never lets them kiss yer
But I'm ok in the stratosphere
I kinda like it up here

But all I can do is fall fall fall fall

It's late Saturday evening and the bar clientele have been up for the gig. Mike Remo has drawn them into the world of 'Skulk Rock' and now they dance with abandon and individuality. Their worldly cares are lifted by the relentless groove and poetry of the songs; assisted by the reduced bar prices courtesy of the venue owner and gig promoter.

Partway through the song a contrasting set of people enter at the back of the room. They look incongruous in the context of the skulk rock audience. James' attention is drawn to them as the women in the group are striking. All the group seem to circulate around one particular woman. She stands out amongst the group. The more James looks, the more he can't seem to take his eyes off her. She blesses him with a momentary eye contact, brief but significant, before looking away to chat to her friends once again. As James regains his stage self he notices Mike Remo looking at him and shaking his head, smiling.

When James looks back to where they were standing they are already leaving. They exit through some rear doors. The stand out girl is last to leave and James watches her hair sway as it reflects the electric lights of the doorway. Did she look back there? She did!

After the gig James is packing equipment away and joking with bandmates.

'Well, we held that audience ok?'

'We sure did – except for the guys at the back – they looked like they beamed onto the wrong planet.'

'Did you see the girl in the red dress?'

Mike Remo pauses and looks across at James.

'Jimmy English your pussy radar was on red alert there', Mike smiles.

'She just caught my eye Mike! That's all.'

Mike Remo affects his Cary Grant accent as he repeats, 'She just caught my eye!'

Thunderman joins in now, 'She never took her eyes off the geetar player Mike!', followed by The Gnome, 'I bet she's got a thing for English accents Mike! What chance have we got?'

James looks up from putting his guitar in its case and sees the three Dirtkickers stood smiling at him. He tries to come up with a witty reply but fails miserably and settles for giving them the finger.

The three Dirtkickers smile and high five each other. The Gnome engages his serious tone now,

'Women like that never stick around! Man, they are wired differently.'

'You should know pal!', James smiles at his minor last word victory.

As they finish loading equipment into the truck James decides he needs to run into the adjacent hotel for a bathroom call before the long journey ahead of them. As he rushes out of the bathroom, as his bandmates wait in the van, he bumps into THE girl.

'Oh shit! Sorry!' (He saves her from falling)

'It's ok!' she smiles.

They look at each other in an embarrassing silence moment.

She breaks the dead air, 'I enjoyed your music.'

'Thanks, but we didn't manage to keep you all in the room.'

She looks at the ceiling

'Peer groups. They wanted to go back to the wedding disco. I enjoy live music though.'

He pauses

'Glad you enjoyed it anyway.'

She smiles

'Where are you playing next?'

'We have a gig tomorrow night in Yuba City and then a couple of bars in Napa. Then back to SF.'

'What are you called?'

'The Lowdown DirtKickers.'

'Alluring name', she smiles, then adds 'Maybe I'll catch you back in SanFrancisco?'

'What's your name?', she adds.

'I'm James.'

'I'm Felicia.'

She lightly kisses him. He is spellbound. As she turns and walks away she stops and turns back momentarily

'Love your accent too!'

She turns the corner and he pauses.

He finds a flyer in his back pocket and walks quickly after her.

Turning the corner, he sees a long long corridor and a thousand doors, no Felicia and no clues.

His band mates sound the horn and he reluctantly exits.

In the van he excitedly tells a bandmate of his encounter.

'Told you they love the Cary Grant accent!', Thunderman laughs. Mike Remo affects an impatient tone, 'Long piss Jimmy, we got miles to make – and you have been on a wild woman chase?'

'Wasn't like that Mike, it was different.'

'Where have I heard that before? Like when I had to rescue you from Texas Tina's husband after he caught you listening to her life story out back?'

Thunderman affects a confused look to The Gnome, 'Can limeys hear with their dicks?'

A question mark appears above The Gnomes head.

James nods and laughs,

'Well that was an error of character judgement on my part and I do owe you my life!'

'Too fucking right young man, you're on this planet to write songs. Don't give me the 'this was different story' ... '

James mutters defiantly

'This WAS fuckin' different ... .'

Mike Remo pulls out a CD, slots it into the car player and sings along.

She's Too Much

https://badpeoplethemusical.bandcamp.com/track/shes-too-much

She got a high class voice
And high class friends
She wawks the dawg
From her Mercedes Benz
She got a sun tan in winter
And she's cool in June
but if you don't flash cash
she don't notice you

She could be my babe and I swear it's true
and I could paddle to mars in my old canoe
She believes in love at first sight
When it makes her rich overnight
Too much for you
she's killed a few
I swear it's true
Her blood is blue
she's got legs so long and heels so high
you need a pilot's licence to look her in the eye
So get your feet back down on the ground

Sophisticated lady
A cheque book baby
She likes gold bars
and movie stars
but if you can't afford the broad
you can't tame the dame
If you ain't got the credit
You'd better forget it

But she could be my babe I swear it's true
and I could take a taxi to Timbuctoo
I could get my head inside her dress
and I believe in life after death
She's too much for you
she's killed a few

I swear it's true
Her blood is blue
she's a power dresser
Your Harley won't impress her
So forget she ever showed and hit the road

The song plays as the Lowdown Dirtkicker van cruises on a starlight highway now. James' thoughts ascend high above the van. For some reason he thinks of his father. He ejects that thought and wonders about his Mum; it's been a while since he wrote. The Gnome and Thunderman doze off. Mike Remo stares ahead at the highway keeping his thoughts to himself. James remains wide awake and watches the stars. He thinks about Felicia. He thinks about Felicia. And then, he thinks about Felicia.

Highway 99

A golden eagle falls from a low slung white cloud meandering across the Montana sky. Far below, Lucy follows a highway as it turns south. She has no idea of time as she white knuckles the steering wheel. Eventually she meets Highway 2 at Saco. Again, it crosses her mind to turn east and maybe head home after all. She quickly discounts that idea. Her mind panics a little as she wonders how much Seth had told his family about her. Did they even know her full name? Did they know she was from Illinois? When she had first met Seth he had told her he was desperate to escape the gravitational pull of his family. Even he seemed scared by the rest of The Snake Family. One time only he had taken her to meet them and the family had virtually ignored her. She hadn't been too worried by that, having found his Dad and two brothers to be scary, bordering on evil. Mrs Snake and his sister AJ seemed withdrawn as if they didn't want to talk to her either. Inwardly Lucy had giggled at his father being called Jake Snake but she didn't giggle upon meeting him. She had been so relieved to get out of the house. She still shivers as she remembers Jake slowly looking her up and down. She reminds herself of how she almost decided to end things with Seth at this point but he had convinced her that he was also trying to distance himself from his family and make a life of his own. So much was unexplained. How did Seth come to have a whole farm to himself when he didn't seem to know anything much at all about farming? At first it was fun together trying to work out what to do and when. Lucy had become enthusiastic, if not a little obsessed even, but most things they tried failed. Eventually Seth would begin to go away for days telling her he had to help on Jake's farm and when he did he would always return with a bundle of cash.

She turns east on Highway 2. She presently arrives in Malta and gasses the Dog before stopping at a diner. Over a meal and coffee she studies the old map book she had taken from the farmhouse and decides to head south on Highway 191. As she starts The Dog she talks to it as if her only friend. 'OK Mr Dog, we're gonna be rollin south on 191.' Leaving Malta the country is dull and depressing but her mood lifts as the sun breaks through and the bump and rise of America now becomes littered with fresh springgreen trees. The Dog rolls obediently.

Lucy can't stop looking in the mirror. The Snakes slither into her mind and she dreads the sight of The Snake Family truck on the road behind her. She fights hard to lock those thoughts away. She dials in the radio and Morrissey's voice suddenly fills the Dog, 'I decree today that life is simply taking and not giving, England is mine and it owes me a living'. She thinks of England. 'What is it like over there?' 'Maybe she'd go over one day, if San Francisco didn't work out?' She couldn't remember when she had decided to head for SF. Maybe sat in the diner in Malta? She had always had an ambition to see Santa Monica one day and hoped music would take her there. Zuma Beach and passing Bob in the street. Who knows? Maybe there were too many people with the same idea though? It had suddenly crystallized in her mind that SF may be a better option? Easier to blend? Easier to find casual work? Not so far? Yes! This was a good plan.

And so, at that moment her masterplan was formed as best she could figure. Head for San Francisco and if that didn't work she'd go to England. She banged the steering wheel and said 'Yes!', clinging to positivity. A voice in her head said 'Not much of a plan Lucy' but she discounts it. She glances in the mirror once more. No Snake Family!!! Surely she could lose herself in SanFrancisco? She daydreamed of a flat on a hill overlooking the bay; she had had enough of wide open spaces.

She cruises through Judith Gap now. Snowcapped mountain ranges visible to the east and to the west. It kind of felt like she was escaping. She took a deep breath. She wondered about Morrissey? She knew he was from Manchester. She knew that if San Francisco wasn't far enough she would head for Manchester England.

She crosses Highway 12 at Harlowtown and continues on 191. After Melville she see tall mountains to the west. Her first glimpse of the rockies. She likes the thought of her insignificance. Her nightmares begin to retreat. At Big Timber she pulls over and gazes over the Yellowstone River. She sleeps in The Dog for a couple of hours. After Big Timber 191 becomes an interstate and she nervously guides The Dog onto the westbound side. She gradually settles into a drive groove as the landscapes and clouds pass. Every mile eases her nerves as she heads due west now.

As she hits Bozeman she suddenly remembers Seth telling her that Gibson Guitars are now made there and she decides to detour into the town for coffee and food. She pulls off and finds herself on Highway 191 again and now it's Main Street. She finds a coffee house and parks. The coffee house is quiet and the waiter is a friendly guy. She finds herself asking what Bozeman is like for work.

'It's ok if you like waitressing!'

'Well I need some money.'

She wonders why she tells that lie as she has liberated a large bundle of notes from one of Seth's draws in the farmhouse and it sits in her rucksack. The thought makes her wonder how much cash was burnt in the fire.

When the waiter returns he asks

'Are you passing through?'

'Yes, I'm going to California.'

She curses herself for the giveaway. What if The Snakes are here asking questions. What if they hire a PI? Her best logic tells her it's unlikely. Her mind returns to the conversation grateful for friendly company.

'Wish I was.'

'Bozeman looks nice to me?'

'I know, but it's small.'

'Don't they make Gibson Guitars here?'

He smiles.

'A lot of people ask that. Four blocks down, turn right and just before the interstate junction on the right.'

'Really?'

'Yup, you into guitars?'

'I used to have a Gibson.'

'Wish I could afford one. Not much hope on the tips here.'

'You into music?'

'Yes, I play and try and make up songs.'

'Me too. I guess that's why I'm heading to California?'

'Can I come?'

Lucy realises he's a nice kid and only joking.

'Sure!'

'Well I wish! I'm getting married in August.'

Lucy smiles at him, 'Congratulations!'

'Thanks. I do play in a band here though.'

'Hope you have a hit record at the same time as me. As long as mine is higher!!'

Lucy smiles as she sees him realise that the conversation is at an end. He repeats,

'Four blocks down, turn right and you pass Gibson on the way back to the Interstate.'

As she leaves the coffee house and drives on down Main Street she sees the sign indicating right to the Interstate. Just as she sees the interstate traffic in the distance, she sees a Gibson sign and finds herself driving into an industrial estate. An autopilot seems to have taken over her mind as she drives into the Gibson car park. She finds herself walking into a foyer and a receptionist looking at her suspiciously.

'Can I help you?'

'Maybe? I have an old Gibson that needs repair.'

The receptionist is efficient and explains that they only make them here. Lucy becomes embarrassed and close to tears for some reason. She pauses holding the counter for support and unaware that a workman is now standing behind her. As Lucy turns away he speaks,

'I'll look at it for you young lady.'

The receptionist looks away as if annoyed her word is not taken as final.

The workman is older but Lucy is glad for his intervention as he seems kind hearted. She smiles at the receptionist as she backs away from the counter. She walks to the car with the workman. She feels herself redden with embarrassment as she opens the passenger door of The Dog and the broken Gibson sits sadly on the passenger seat. The old man looks at her with compassion,

'That's a pretty messed up guitar young lady!'

Lucy can't stop the tears arriving. The old man comforts her, 'Hey take it easy. There have been worse accidents?'

'My Dad gave it me.'

'What happened to it?'

'Drunken boyfriend.'

'Leave him!'

'I did.'

'I'd kill him for that!'

'I d …oooon't fancy the state penitentiary one little bit!!!', she giggles between tears. Inwardly she admonishes herself for blabbing.

'Any judge would let you off!', he tries to cheer her up.

The old guy looks at the guitar.

'A Nick Lucas! Don't see many of these. Not this old.'

Lucy wipes her eyes. He continues

'13 frets to the body; or what's left of it! Wow! These are rare indeed. Early 30s I bet. Bob Dylan played one of these! His was repaired too.'

Lucy smiles at him. He asks, 'Where do you live?'

'I'm just passing through on my way to California.'

'If you can stick around for a week I'll find a body for it. We do reissues of these at the moment. New ones are 14 frets to the body so it will take me some time to sort things out for the pin bridge but this neck is still ok.' He thinks out loud. Lucy gathers herself.

Lucy is glad of his company and for the first time in days she feels not quite so all alone. Her tears return.

'I can pay.'

'Hey young lady, I never mentioned money! I CAN do this.'

'Really?'

'Yes, really. Do you have somewhere to stay?'

She thinks and slowly shakes her head.

'No.'

'Can you bake and drive a sewing machine?'

'Errrrm yes, well I can try?'

'Well my wife is drowning in preparations for our grandaughter's wedding and we could sure use some help on the cake and bunting?'

Lucy looks at him and her tears return yet again.

'Do we have a deal?'

She gathers herself, 'We sure do!'

'GGGGreat!', he smiles and hugs her, 'I'm Howard Smith.'

Lucy smiles, 'I'm Lucy Smith.'

'I guess that seals our bargain Lucy Smith!'

Howard drives and Lucy follows. He drives slowly and they head south into town again and then west back on the 191. Lucy thinks the 191 is her favourite highway ever!

Just before Four Corners, Howard turns right and she follows him into a rural area. Eventually he turns along an overgrown track between trees, along a miniature valley to a secluded homestead. Mrs Smith appears on the porch. She is all smiles. Howard gives her a hug. He introduces Lucy and they invite her into the house. Elizabeth Smith is a perfect match for Howard and Lucy slowly begins to relax, especially as Elizabeth seems to love the idea of assistance with her wedding preparations.

'Little Molly is nervous about her Grandma making her wedding cake but somehow I want to do it', Elizabeth explains over dinner.

'Saves money too!', adds Howard.

'Always a good idea!', Lucy agrees.

Lucy hungrily tucks into the stew pie that Elizabeth serves. She doesn't take any persuasion to have a second helping either. Elizabeth looks at her, 'How long since you had a good meal young lady?'

'A while.'

The Smiths look at her. Howard breaks the silence, 'Will that truck get you to California young lady?',

'I hope so. I'll sell it when I get there.'

Howard seems to formulate a next question but stops himself asking it. He glances at Elizabeth. Elizabeth ends the silence, 'Tomorrow we can go to town and get some bunting material? And then we can get to work?' Howard and Elizabeth smile as they watch Lucy finish off her second helping of pie with relish.

*

As Lucy awakes next morning the sunlight dances across her room. She hears the birds sing outside and goes downstairs to find Elizabeth making coffee. Beams of sunlight into the large rustic kitchen, the smell of cooking and freshly brewed coffee leads Lucy to think of her failures on the farm over the last two years. They sit and chat as Lucy tells Elizabeth about her family back in Illinois.

'How come you are out in Montana?', Elizabeth asks.

'I met a guy.'

'It didn't work out?'

'Not quite!'

'What did he do?'

'Not a lot, but he was a talented musician.'

'You play music too?'

'Yes, I guess that's what took me to the Gibson factory.'

'They been good to Howard. He loves his work.'

'I can tell.'

They pause. Lucy continues,

'I'm really grateful for your help.'

'Oh grateful nothing! He's taken your guitar to work and it will keep him out from under my feet. Meanwhile, young lady, we have work to do!'

The days pass and Lucy and Elizabeth lose themselves in their projects. It turns out that Lucy has quite a talent for decorative icing. She loses her self in the wedding cake preparations. Elizabeth's workroom is set up for sewing and they devise a means for mass producing cloth bunting. They create yards and yards and yards of it. Days pass unnoticed. Lucy helps Howard with his vegetable gardens in the evenings.

A week or so later Lucy sees Howard arrive home and take a guitar case out of his truck. She recognises a feeling of sadness as she realises it's her guitar and it will mean that her stay here is coming to an end. Nevertheless, she shakes with excitement as Howard opens up the case on the kitchen table and Lucy sees her old guitar reissued. She recognises the neck and gasps at the quality of the workmanship of the new body. The sunburst similar but not quite as patinated as the original. It's tuned and she sits and rings a G chord. It shimmers and sings. She looks at Howard,

'I can never thank you enough!'

'I enjoyed doing it young Lucy. I have worked on these reissued and we are lucky that the neck joint was a perfect fit. All's I had to do was move the bridge position a little and add some bracing. Could be that that's changed the sound a little but she sounds ok to me!'

'She sure does Howard', Lucy kisses him on the cheek.

Howard blushes and smiles, 'Don't you never hook up with any guitar smashing men in future!'

'I won't be doing that Howard!'

There's a silence before Howard adds, 'I mean it!'

Lucy nods.

*

It turns out that young Molly and Neil are coming over on the following Sunday and Howard and Elizabeth insist that Lucy stays on to meet them. She helps Elizabeth finish wedding preps on the Saturday and then the meal for Sunday. Molly turns out to be the image of Elizabeth and Neil turns out to be the waiter from the coffee shop in Bozeman. They all enjoy the sunny day with a beer and a meal. Sometimes everything just sits right. Lucy again realises how she has wasted the last 2 or 3 years and in the back of her mind she curses The Snakes. Why couldn't they have been like the Smiths? A theory that all Smiths are good people runs in her mind until she reminds herself that she has recently killed someone. She is the black sheep of the Smiths. Guilt runs over her in waves during the dinner.

*

On the Monday morning she is up early to say bye to Howard and Elizabeth before Howard has to leave for work. She's bought him a new embroidered shirt that Elizabeth had mentioned when they were in town. For Elizabeth she's bought an antique necklace to go with the dress she plans to wear for the wedding. They seem genuinely happy to have received the gifts.

Howard brings out a box.

'We have something for you too Lucy.'

He gives her the box and Howard and Elizabeth look on as she opens it to reveal a 5 shot snub nose Smith and Wesson revolver. Lucy looks up in shock. Howard interrupts before she can speak,

'We know there can be trouble in this world young lady. So make sure you take care and protect yourself. Remember what I told you! No guitar smashing boyfriends.'

Lucy promises she will ensure that situation does not arise

ever again.

Elizabeth tells her to come back and see them one day.

Howard painstakingly gives her directions for a quiet short cut back to Highway 90 before he has to leave for work. He tells her she will enjoy the scenery. He seems almost emotional as he then quickly leaves for work. Elizabeth explains that Howard never did like long goodbyes. She hugs Lucy now and pleads with her to be careful. She promises she will and that she will write them when she is safely in San Francisco. She reluctantly opens the driver door of The Dog and climbs in. As she drives slowly away she sees Elizabeth waving until The Dog disappears around a bend. Lucy steals herself to concentrate once again on driving. She takes the route that Howard has described figuring that it will be quiet and give her time to get into the way of driving once more.

Once again there is vacant Highway laid out in front of her. Monumental American scenery in front and to each side. The highway relentless as it leads to a massive rock butte. Lucy sings to herself and the truck,

'How we gonna climb outta here Mr Dog?'

As she gets closer, the highway turns to a dirt road and begins to zig and zag and hairpin its way up the almost sheer face of the landform. She talks to the truck and taps it wheel,

'C'mon The Dog, we can do this together …'

At the top she stops and parks. Her gaze tracks along the horizon as she looks out over the flatlands she has traversed. She sees a dust trail from a vehicle travelling at speed far below and looks nervously at it. She sighs with relief as the dirt road it travels meets the highway and it turns away from her.

She travels on and rejoins Highway 90. The spring sunlight and blue sky is interrupted by a rogue black cloud. The cloud ushers The Snakes back into her mind. She grips the steering wheel of The Dog and presses on the gas tensely. She decides to put miles between her and Montana. She tries to think of Howard and Elizabeth but The Snakes slither and crawl. She looks over at Howard's gift sat on the passenger seat now. Did he know she was in deep trouble? Were Howard and Elizabeth some kind of rogue angels? Lucy enters a drive trance. The scenery of the rockies passes by as she stares at the road ahead. Missoula, Coeur D'Alene and Post Falls before she passes the Washington State Line. As the sign passes she feels some of her tension lift. She finds an anonymous motel and spends a tired evening looking at her map book. She decides to cut south west to Portland and then towards the coast the following day.

'At least I want to see the ocean before I die', she sings to herself, 'Before my veins run dry.'

She plays with chord sequences on the Nick Lucas and thinks of her Dad and Howard. Why aren't all men like that?

Next day she is up and away early. She crosses Snake River at Pasco and somehow its name shocks her. She dare not look at the Snake River to her right now. If she does she sees Seth walking on the water, his skin grey and burnt but blood gushing from his head and chest. She manages to banish him from her mind as she reaches Wallula and sees a sign denoting the waterway as the Columbia River now. She breathes a long sigh of relief. Highway 30 follows the mighty Columbia River and, slowly, she grows to love its magnificence. It is truly irresistible. She convinces herself it has swept Seth away. The highway guides her through the Cascade Mountains and she reluctantly bids farewell to the river at Corbett. It's late when she passes through Portland and the city is asleep. She panics in the town but holds it together watching the magnetic compass on the Dog dashboard top. She keeps heading west until she miraculously hits Highway 99 and follows a sign for south, 'South is good' she tells herself. Gripping tight to the steering wheel the Highway takes her over Ross Island Bridge before swinging south again. She feels good. She decides to stick with Highway 99, she likes the sound of it. She remembers her Dad telling her that 99 starts in Mexico and runs right on up to Alaska (she also remembers him saying 'it's THE most dangerous Highway', although she does remember that that's mainly due to the frozen stretches up in Alaska). She figures she will stick with 99 as long as it heads south west. Like a true friend, it doesn't deviate and it doesn't let her down The old school magnetic compass is her friend too and it keeps saying south west. Gradually the city fades and green fields appear. She sings 'Highway 99 runs right up to the sky' to herself, liking the sound of that. She follows 99 until it becomes Highway 18 just past McMinnville. She laughs at her Dad and his unreliable stories but she knew 18 was good from her previous mapbook studies. She says thankyou in her mind to

Highway 99 and sings to herself 'Your conscience can explode on Highway 99.' Still singing the tune though, she now follows Highway 18 until she hits Highway 101. 101 had been in her mind since she saw it following the Pacific coastline on her map book. She bangs The Dog's steering wheel as if she had discovered the new world. 'Yes yes YES – we made it! We crossed the immensity', she sees herself as a female Jack Kerouac. She cruises into Lincoln City and as she catches her first view of the Pacific Ocean on her right she sees a Motel to the left. She pulls in and gets a room. Lucy is 'Dog Tired' but can't resist a walk on the beach. It's been years since she was on a beach and that was with her family on Lake Michigan. She remembered thinking 'if this is a lake I wanna see the Pacific Ocean.' She isn't disappointed as the fresh air tumbles into her lungs and the rollers boom onto the sand. Her hair blows behind her and the wind seems to blow the shadows and doubts from her mind. As she treks back over soft sand she sees a sign saying 'Oregon State: Tsunami Warning Advice ... .Make for High Ground'. She smiles at it as 'pretty obvious advice' but mostly because it confirms she is now two states from Montana. It eases her mind. She hopes the Motel management will wake her if there is an incoming Tsunami; if not it would solve all her problems for sure.

*

Lucy sleeps with road dreams running in her mind. Her epic journey to the coast replays in its grandeur. The Rockies, The Cascades, The mighty Columbia river. Morrissey and the Smiths. She wakes and stares at the ceiling. She thinks of Howard and Elizabeth. She walks out to a nearby diner for breakfast and hears the ocean between lulls in the road traffic from Highway 101. She almost feels happy as she walks back. On the way back she suddenly gets nervous about her guitar and her 'belongings' which she has left in the room but as she rushes back in her guitar is still there. She opens her rucksack and Howard's gift is still in the box on top. She sighs with relief.

She takes out Nick Lucas and experiments with chords until she finds a nice groove. She absent mindedly begins singing the Highway 99 song she had sung to herself the previous night on the road out of Portland. She begins to jot it down in her notebook. Finishing the song takes most of the morning and she decides there is a good vibe to Lincoln City and she will stay another night.

She checks with reception and decides it's safe to leave her stuff in the room while she takes a walk around the town. She finds a tempting little café and takes lunch there, as usual selecting a secluded corner. On the table a flyer for 'English Bob's Open Mic Night' takes her attention. She asks the waitress where it is and is directed to a bar on the street corner.

'Is English Bob really English?'

'Well he talks real funny – but he's a nice guy. He plays the saxophone.'

'Sounds different!'

'Oh yes, they are a strange set but quite few people turn out on a Monday and they are nice and friendly. You could go along tonight.'

'Will English Bob let me sing?'

'As long as you let him play saxophone with you he will let anyone play.'

Lucy giggles to herself as she had lost track of the days and hadn't realised that today was Monday.

'Thanks, I might.'

Lucy orders 'English Fish and Chips' and thinks 'maybe I will move to England if SF don't work out?'

That afternoon she finishes her Highway 99 song, rehearses it and decides she will try out the song and the 're-issued' Nick Lucas at the open mic. As she re-sings it she remembers how easy it is to memorise her own lyrics. She has always found it that way, she can remember lyrics from lots of older songs from her childhood too. Her own songs are even easier to remember.

*

As she walks into the bar that evening a gangly eccentric older guy sees her and immediately gangles across towards her.

'Hello, not seen you here before. Welcome!'

His accent gives away his identity as English Bob.

'You must be Bob?'

'Errrrm, affirmative! How did you know?'

Lucy smiles, 'Your reputation precedes you!'

'Indeed it does young lady. I'm famous as a noise nuisance around here!'

English Bob smiles and Lucy feels at ease in his company.

'Can I play a song?'

'Of course you can young lady.'

English Bob gives her a free drink token and recommends the IPA bitter.

'I'll put you on when there's a few more people in.'

English Bob hesitates, 'Errrrm, can I play Sax with you?'

'Of course you can young man!'

English Bob beams a smile and gives her another beer token.

The IPA beer tastes good to Lucy as she relaxes and looks around the bar. She feels comfortably anonymous. Would be performers drift into the bar carrying their various musical instruments. English Bob makes each and every one of them welcome. She remembers her times on the open mic circuit in her home town. She has much to be grateful to guys like English Bob for. If they didn't make the effort to host open-mic nights she might never have got started in music. She mentally raises a glass to English Bob and his like. She remembers how she learnt more about performing than she ever did in music lessons at school. Firstly, if you want to perform an original song, you have to have an original song; she learned to complete a song and learn it this way. And then, when you get the stage at an open mic it's your gig. You have to do something to get attention. She had tried it all. Singing loud, singing quiet, inserting swear words into lyrics. She'd even put violence into lyrics and now she questioned if she really was a violent person. Of course she was. Guilty as charged. Events had proved it. The vision of dead Seth zombies back into her mind. It lets in the rest of The Snakes and she finds herself trying to banish visions of them hurtling west in pursuit. She takes a few large swallows of her IPA and watches English Bob nervously looking at his watch before commencement.

It had been at a night like this when she had first met Seth. His dark brown eyes had danced as he sang and played guitar. All those tricks you could try weren't necessary for Seth. His voice just carried you to another world. It's just not possible to define what it is that gives certain people that ability. Can you learn it? She had been captivated by it. Too captivated and imprisonment had obviously not rehabilitated her had it? She had fucking killed him. Her body shudders as she remembers the gunshots. The ringing in her ears.

Her thoughts spiral downwards. If only Seth had not shown her how to use the gun; not that it would take much working out; any 'shit-for-brains-piece-of-shit-fucked-up-arsehole' could manage that. The whole history of the world proves that theorem. A voice brings her back from the darkness; English Bob has sat down next to her,

'I didn't get our name young lady?'

'It's Lu ... (she pauses) ... cinda.'

Bob looks at her somewhat quizzically, 'Well it's nice to meet you Lucinda.'

Bob looks around the room and then at his list. He taps his pencil onto his pad, deep in thought, eventually reaching a decision, 'There is Blue Andy and then the Hot Banjos. I'll put you on then if that's ok?'

Lucy smiles and nods. She feels nervous tension begin to take over. It's a feeling she knows but this time she welcomes it as it takes her mind off the darkness.

Blue Andy rattles through some blues tunes. He is an accomplished guitar player; far more dextrous than she could ever be. He plays an old telecaster through a Fender Tweed amp to create an authentic overdriven sound. Lucy makes a mental note to buy herself a telecaster when she eventually makes herself some money out of music. That could be a long old time for sure. She fantasises over old guitars. Telecasters look so unglamorous. A nice road worn one would be perfect. Dunno though, aren't they quite a long scale? Her hands are not that big. She imagines herself in front of the mirror trying on various guitars. She laughs at her vanity. 'Well I'm a fierce cold eyed killer. A bit of vanity is of marginal significance!'

The Hot Banjos are a guitar, banjo and fiddle trio. They play some intricate instrumental tunes and Lucy feels good about following them. She feels even better as she takes the stage. It's been a while since she's been here and now she remembers the buzz. Bob plugs a lead into Nick Lucas and Lucy checks her favourite G-chord. She mentally thanks Howard and her thoughts return momentarily to Howard and Elizabeth's house and garden. She smiles to herself.

Lucy elects to stand rather than sit; she always prefers that. She also knows that girls are at an advantage at open mics as the bulk of the clientele are men who want to demonstrate their guitar skills but she figures girls can open a song up easier. TeeHee, she also knows that men are always attracted to girls with guitars. Sure enough, as Lucy begins the song the audience begin to pay attention. A group of guys at the bar put their conversation on hold and she sees their faces half turn to face her; as if to give her a chance to gain their attention-favour. She relishes the challenge. The 'fuck you' facet of her character swells under the influence of the IPA no doubt.

There's a definite 'sigh' from the audience as English Bob straps on his saxophone and moves to the other mic. Lucy smiles at him. She asks him not to play until part way through the song. She IS Bruce and he IS Clarence, to her it's a good omen.

Highway 99

https://badpeoplethemusical.bandcamp.com/track/highway-99

There is a mountaintop in Sausalito
That I go to when I get low
I like to know how high I can go
Like a saint climbin' on his halo
I like the air that – that you get – up there
And there's an alien in my window
And I'm not scared but
It's definitely a close encounter – The Director's Cut
And I'm not scared – but they are – everywhere
Give me a sabre of light
I don't have much energy tonight

Just like the nights with no curtains
- in our railroad room
We always knew for certain
- we would fight off the gloom
We were the sentries – of the darkest night
And I thought I'd never consider this
– but here I am
Never thought I could (take this risk) steal this kiss
well maybe I can
I won't give in – without a fight

Night dreams are easy tonight
The answer to my selfish plight
And Highway 99 runs right up to the sky
But you will cry and you can die - on Highway 99
Armies of angels assemble - right under this moon
And holy empires crumble - and about time too
Some debts the taxman never collects - it's true
Like I never declared - that I still love you

A Yokohama fog falls and curls
Canadian snow lies over the world
The old ice ages wait their turn
Summer sunshine burns
An armada of anger - is anchored off Stavanger
A Sargasso Sea of sorrow - could smother all tomorrows
The Kerry rain - runs down my lane
It's time to decide if I will ride - on Highway 99
She sleeps in Seattle and she could be mine
There's nowhere to hide
Virginia plains - are my domain.

I should take any other road - not Highway 99
There's many other ways I know - not Highway 99
I really love the scenery - on Highway 99
There are dark and deep ravines - on Highway 99
It is the most dangerous road - Highway 99
Where your conscience can explode - Highway 99
A year can pass in just a day - on Highway 99
Your whole life can slip away - on Highway 99
There are so many wrecks - on Highway 99
Am I gonna be the next? - on Highway 99
Well what do you expect? - on Highway 99
There is no life after death on Highway 99

There's good applause for the song and English Bob beams. Lucy carefully packs Nick Lucas away and thanks Bob.

'NO! Thank you Lucinda. You're the first acoustic artist that gave me some space. Sadly the saxophone is not as popular as it used to be.'

Lucy is struck by the sincerity of his words. Perhaps the base human instinct to be creative is what sets them apart from other species? It's a good theory.

Bob gives her a third beer token. That seals his place in her mind. 'Arise Sir Bob!' She puts him nobly into her army of angels. If the darkness keeps coming she is going to have some considerable allies as she goes down fighting. It's a sign!

She giggles. She has always loved beer philosophy and so she walks over to the bar and cashes a token, grateful to have got through her first performance for what must be months. She sits and listens as more local artists get their weekly fix of playing live. Lucy finds things to enjoy in most of the songs and performers. She thinks to herself 'Lucinda – Tsk!' She laughs as the IPA circulates in her blood.

As the evening progresses, English Bob seems to tire of blowing hard to be heard above the louder bands that now play and he comes over to chat. 'Lucinda' is glad of the company.

'I've heard Route 66 and Highway 51 and Highway 61 Revisited – but I've never heard Highway 99 Lucinda?'

'I only made it up yesterday Bob.'

'Wow, an original! I enjoyed it.'

'Thanks Bob and thanks for your instrumental breaks.'

Bob smiles

'We should form a duo?'

'I'm only passing through Bob.'

'Where are you going?'

'San Francisco, to see if there's any opportunities for would be singer songwriters.'

'I'm sure there will be for you young lady.'

'I'm not so sure Bob. Music is tough and I've been out of the big swim for a few years.'

'Well if it doesn't work out come back and we can form that duo! Lincoln City is ok if you like a quiet life.'

Bob's flirting is kind of cute and Lucy is quite glad of his attentions. She needs friends for sure. Friends who'll wield their weapons in her defence, magnified by love, when the forces of darkness come for her. Beacons of light in battlefields. She conjures a vision of Bob on a white horse wielding a mighty sword and slicing the heads off snakes around his horse; the arc of his blade flashing in the face of moonlight. Christ – she had better lay off the IPA shit?

'English Bob, we could even go back to England? What's it like over there?'

'Grim. I come from Manchester and, to be frank, I much prefer it over here.'

'Isn't it a little quiet up here in Oregon?'

'Yes but after 35 years in a foundry and being made redundant and finally having some money, I decided to get some fresh air.'

Bob draws in a deep breath and affects a posh English accent, 'Pin in a map brought me here young lady!'

'Good for you Bob. Must have taken some degree of courage?'

'Well it worked out ok so far. Would be even better if I could share my time with a good woman?'

Bob smiles hopefully and Lucy smiles back, 'Well if I was 30 years older Bob I would jump at the chance.'

Bob immediately looks hurt and Lucy feels shitty for the crass remark. He sounds hurt as he replies,

'I hope you didn't think I was making advances Lucinda! And, anyway, you are a married woman!'

Lucy is shocked, 'I'm fucking not!'

Bob waves his 3rd finger and points at her left hand.

Lucy realises she still has the gold ring Seth gave her on it. Oh shit! She is unnerved by the moment. Panicking inside. She fakes laughter and explains,

'My ex bought me that and it didn't fit any other finger!'

Bob sounds unconvinced, 'Ah ok, my apologies.'

Lucy calms herself and leans across to hold his hand, 'We finished rather suddenly and I have been in a strange place ever since.'

Bob is convinced by her tone this time.

'I forgot it was on my finger.'

Lucy suddenly realised why Howard and Elizabeth had stopped their questions suddenly. 'Fuck, fuck fuck!', she thought to herself. Bob breaks the awkward silence.

'Are you around tomorrow night Lucinda?'

'I hadn't thought Bob, why?'

'I'm going down to Lincoln Beach for their fortnightly open mic. We could do a couple of songs?'

Lucy feels unable to refuse having been found guilty of insulting remarks and unkind suspicion.

'I'd love to Bob. Thanks!'

Bob smiles, the spikiness banished forever.

Lucy knows she trusts him implicitly now. One the noblest knights of her realm. 'What an honour that is?'

They arrange to meet up at Bob's house the following afternoon and run through a couple of songs, Lucy finishes her IPA as other musos begin to 'doughnut' around her and Bob. They are keen to talk music and, The Snakes are banished to the extreme outer territories of her mind. She hears herself laughing. The witness Lucy Smith stands outside herself watching. Almost happy for her counterpart. 'Live for the moment Lucy Smith – You're an existentialist!'

This Ring Is A Bullet

Lucy Smith and Nick Lucas stagger across Lincoln City, guided by instinct and IPA, to the seclusion of the motel room. She inwardly curses and admonishes herself.

'Shit shit shit Ms Low-Profile! Lucinda? Lucinda!!!!? English Bob is probably searching for me under Most Wanted by now?'

She sits on the bed and giggles a little to herself,

'Not sure you'll make a serial killer Lucy Smith. Maybe best leave it at one?'

She looks at the ring on her finger and tries to remove it. The ring stubbornly refuses to slide over her finger joint. She tells herself not to panic and goes to the bathroom and applies some soap to the problem. Eventually the ring passes over her knuckle joint and she breathes a major relief sigh. She places it on the bedside cabinet and quickly falls to sleep.

Maybe it was the IPAs or her general predicament, but strange dreams rule the night. Eagles fly over the Rockies. So high they can see the western ocean in the setting sun. One dives downwards through mountain peaks and the valleys crawling with snakes. Suddenly the snakes part for a much larger snake to pass, slithering at speed towards the ocean. Lucy wakes in a cold sweat.

She stares at the ring on the bedside cabinet. It becomes a problem in her mind until she puts it to one side and goes to motel reception where breakfast is served. She sits alone trying not to think.

As she returns to her room a storm blows in. She makes a coffee. She surfs quickly through some news channels dreading to hear an item about murder and arson in Montana; Nationwide police hunt; APB Ms Lucy Smith. She turns the TV off with a vengeance. She decides to re-pack her rucksack, putting the box containing Howard's revolver and the ring from her bedside table onto the kingsize bed counterpane. She stares at them both in bewilderment. They remind her of recent dark history. She sees Howard's kind demeanour and Seth's leer and wonders which of the seven days of creation gave rise to God creating this range of human behaviour. She shudders, muttering to herself, 'Heavy metal – cold steel, gold and lead. Which is heaviest? Gold I bet?' She thinks of her Dad and how he used to try and teach her about the Periodic Table of the elements

The rain now lashes against the small window as if trying to get in. Lucy takes out Nick Lucas. She looks at the ring and the gun and notices that Howard has even put a box of shells in the gift box. Nick Lucas gives her a little chordy riff and she sings to herself, 'this ring is a bullet … '

It's enough to kick start her and she takes out her notebook. Time blurs and a ghost visits. When it lets Lucy return she stares down at her notebook. The song is complete. She sings it to herself thinking, 'This is a keeper!'

Although the song seems dark, the happy feeling of having created something overrides the darkness and somehow enables her push away even darker thoughts.

This Ring Is A Bullet

https://badpeoplethemusical.bandcamp.com/track/this-ring-is-a-bullet

All the jewellery you bought me
Well I don't want it
I don't even want the money
If I ever pawn it

This ring is a bullet

This bracelet is a snake
A snake round my arm
Venom in my veins
You did me nothing but harm

This ring is a bullet
It put a hole in my heart
Don't you argue don't you start
If I had a trigger – I would pull it
This ring is a bullet

Gold is heavy metal
It only drags you down
Like a summer flower's petals
Lying on the ground

This ring is a bullet
It put a hole in my heart
Don't you argue don't you start
If I had a trigger – I would pull it
This ring is a bullet

As she finishes the song Lucy thinks to herself, 'Wow, two finished songs in 2 days! I should kill people more often?'

She hopes she's joking and she tries to think of good things. Her Mum, her Dad, Howard and Elizabeth … .English Bob. Everyone has a dark side?

'We all got a dark side
We try to hide
Ain't it just like the night?…'

She stops herself from beginning yet another song.

By lunch time the storm has passed leaving grey-black streak-clouds across a distant sky. Lucy decides to put her song lyrics into action and try to pawn the ring. The motel receptionist directs her to the relevant part of town. She soon finds a suitable 'Antique Mart' and gets offered 75 bucks for the ring. She knows it's probably a bad deal but she thinks of her lyric. She takes the money. She explores her way back to the Motel, picks up Nick Lucas and then follows her directions over to Bob's house.

Bob has a small but well maintained garden. It's enclosed and provides a pleasant surrounding as they share a beer and potatoes and stew Bob has prepared. Lucy asks him about England. Bob tells her about the suburbs of Manchester where he grew up. He tells her of green valleys and rainy days. English football and cricket. Jazz music and then rock and roll and then rock music. He talks at length about The Chris Barber Band and how jazz and skiffle music was king when he was young.

'Oh, they brought American blues artists over to England Lucinda. I remember the excitement of seeing Muddy Waters. I saw Howling Wolf too back in those days too. The Chris Barber Band are so dear to me Lucinda. Do you know that Chris Barber and Pat Halcox, his trumpet player, have played together touring for longer than any other partnership in music. The success those guys deserve was kind of taken away from them by the rise of the pop bands but they are still working and touring to this day. I love those guys; always did and I always will.'

Lucy nods as she listens to Bob's reminiscenses, his eyes vacant as his memory reels run and run. She sees bittersweet memories in his eyes and doesn't want to interrupt his flow.

'I worked in a steelworks at the time and spent long long weeks pulling red hot steel bars across the factory floor. It was called a "rolling mill" and they used to pour the molten steel into chrome plated cooled moulds. We had to grab the hot bars with tongs and pull them across to the cooling bath. They would bite you if they got chance. We used to call them The Snakes.'

Mention of 'The Snakes' set Lucy's mind into red alert and she visibly jumps, Bob pauses before continuing,

'If someone on the floor lost control of their snake you had to be ready to dance. They were such long long weeks and I used to think music all the time. Wishing my time away for work to finish and then waiting for Fridays when we could get out to local jazz gigs or even take the train into Manchester itself.'

Lucy idly remarks, 'Sounds like happy days Bob?'

'NO! I used to hate every moment on the floor of the rolling mill Lucy. Hot, dangerous and fumes everywhere. Prison would've been easier. I should've escaped sooner.'

He stares vacantly into space. Lucy sees lines appear on his face,

'I had a steady girlfriend but she lost interest in music and wanted us to buy a bungalow in another town. I guess she wanted all the modern gadgets and stuff but I just wanted to carry on going out at the weekends. Took me too long to learn my lessons and she was gone.'

His eyes close momentarily, 'Don't EVER work in a factory Lucinda it steals your soul 5 days a week. I've seen grown men cry. Music could be one way out but it was a cruel business too. You need the talent or you need to be lucky enough to find a band with talented people. I used to play in a trad band back around

Manchester in the sixties', a sadness in his voice, 'but the times were changing I was a fossil even then Lucinda!'

Lucy feels confident enough with Bob now and tells him, 'I'm really Lucy. Not sure why I said my name was Lucinda.'

Bob snaps out of his memory-dreams and looks thoughtful for a moment.

'Not as if I go through the wanted posters young lady!'

She feigns a laugh but inwardly wonders if The Snake Family will actually engage the law. She hopes not, pinning the hope on her memories of Seth telling her of their hatred of law enforcement officers. She changes the subject back to music,

'Is that why you learned the saxophone Bob?'

'Kind of. My love of music goes back to my Dad and his incessant playing of what he used to call "LP Records"' His old record player was his pride and joy. He had an LP for all the musicals.'

'OMG, my Dad used to play those old records too Bob. He always told me that his uncle would play them all the time when he was a boy!'

Bob smiles at his memories, 'I used to love Carousel.'

He breaks into 'If I loved you – words wouldn't come in an easy way ... .'

When he stops, Lucy sings, 'When I marry Mr Snow ... .'

Bob beams, surprised that someone so much younger knows the song.

'You can't not mention "When you walk through a storm ..." Can you?'

Lucy shakes her head in unequivocal agreement, 'What a song!!!!'

'South Pacific?' – they ostentatiously sing 'Bally Hiiiiiiii.'

'The King and I' – 'Getting to know you.'

'My Fair Lady?' – 'I have often walked – down that street before.'

'Brigadoon?' – 'Is Scotland really a magical place Bob?'

'No, it's a shithole Lucy. Full of Jocks.'

'Jocks?', she looks confused.

'It's what we call people from Scotland.'

'Like we call you Limeys?'

'Yeh – similar. I've not been called that for a while though Lucy!'

'You don't like Jocks?'

'Well Great Britain is full of rivalries – these things can easily get out of hand – I think it's more that they don't like the English?'

'Well, I like Limeys Bob. You and Morrissey for starters!'

Bob smiles again as Lucy continues, 'I once made up a song about my Dad and his love of musicals.'

'Well we must do that one at the open mic tonight?'

Lucy smiles and nods. She thinks of her Dad dancing around their front room as he played old musical soundtrack albums on his ancient record player.

They finish their meal and then get around rehearsing the song. The process clears Lucy's mind of her problems and she feels relaxed.

When it is time to go Bob gets his car from his double garage. Lucy waits on the drive as Bob reverses out in a Ford Mustang.

'Wow Bob, nice wheels.'

'Motor vehicles and music are my weaknesses Lucy.'

'Good weaknesses Bob!'

They put Nick Lucas and Bob's Saxophone on the rear seat and Lucy feels the thrust from the passenger seat into her back as English Bob gives a 'YeeHaaaaa' blasts off into the sea air. Bob tells Lucy of his liking for American Highways and vehicles. 'I have a Harley Davidson Fat Boy too that I like to use in summer. You only live once Lucy and I started late.' The drive down the coast is relaxing for Lucy as Bob enthuses about his Mustang and his Harley and his old Yamaha YTS Tenor. Lucy enjoys his enthusiasm. As she tells him about her plans for San Francisco Bob tells her how he bought his Harley from a garage down there. She tells him that she will be selling The Dog when she gets there and asks if he has any advice.

'Oh man Lucy, you should go and see Marv at Marv's Motors. He's part hippie, part Hell's Angel, part Muso and, although he's been around the block a bit, he will give you a fair deal.'

'Thanks Bob, don't let me leave without getting his details offof you', she continues, 'Is he trustworthy?'

Bob pauses in thought, eventually concluding, 'I would say so.'

'Good because The Dog is old and I'd prefer it if the last owner couldn't ever trace it.'

Bob gives Lucy a suspicious look and then a knowing smile, 'Marv is your man Lucy. He cut me good deals with both my vehicles.'

Bob takes an inland detour from Highway 101 into the hills and enjoys showing off his mustang. There's a silence as Lucy takes in the coastal scenery and then as they pass through a nature reserve.

'Nice car English Bob.'

'Marv's Motors: Keeps America Rolling!'

Lucy smiles at his enthusiasm.

'I'll sure go and see Marv when I get to SF Bob, thanks.'

Bob promises to give Marv a ring and tell him to cut her a good deal.

They arrive at the venue and Lucy enjoys meeting Bob's assembly of eccentric friends. Wangly Dangly, Boris The Cranium and Adrian The Alien. They all have drinks and are deep in conversation about crazy physics. Boris has a theory that is supposed to unify the forces of gravity and electromagnetism. From what she can gather, Boris has developed an idea that all atoms get distorted a little to turn them to really really small magnets. If you put two bodies near to each other the billions of little magnets switch so that it creates a really really weak force which is gravity.

'Not so weak if you jump off the Empire State Boris?'

'Ah but; everything is relative you know!'

Boris rattles on about relativity now. It makes Lucy think of her Dad. It mostly washes over her head but she loves their company and their enthusiasm. She asks Boris if he could make her a time machine.

'You've got your whole life ahead of you young lady!. No need to turn back time and you don't want to rush forward.'

Lucy gets a little spiky about being called Young Lady, 'You're the millionth person to call me "Young Lady" Boris The Cranium!!!'

English Bob diffuses the spikiness but looks concernedly at Lucy. Lucy senses his concern and smiles, 'well we all make mistakes it would be good to go back and correct.'

Boris The Cranium informs, 'hmmmm,that would contravene the laws of physics as presently understood. But, for you Young … .(he stops himself) Lucy I shall see if I cant extend my latest theories.'

Lucy laughs and thanks him. She doesn't notice English Bob looking at her with some concern.

Boris is talking to himself now. 'hmmmmm, what if Einstein was actually wrong and the speed of light can be exceeded? Just because his relativistic formulations reduce to Newton at low speeds just how much do we actually use Einstein in this context? We know he was wrong with his Cosmological Constant so what if there was another error? After all, it's a big assumption to pull from thin air? Like Planck, where the fuck did he get that from? Just a mathematical artifice to help the jigsaw fit Miss Lucy. That's the thing you see, the only truth we have is math. That's what they should tell kids at school. Not make them do exercises. Math is our window into the world and the universe outside. Or maybe many universes? Never mind the religious texts. Prophets only tell you lies!', Boris begins to rant.

Wangly gets some more beers in and places an IPA in front of Boris as he is lost in thought now. They all smile.

The compere calls English Bob and Lucy to the stage. This audience seem disinterested. It's a good feeling for Lucy because it somehow fortifies her confidence once again. The 'I'll show these fuckers!' mentality takes hold. She looks across at English Bob and nods. They perform Lucy's Highway 99 song and follow it with their rehearsed song about the old musicals.

Lucy introduces it,

'This song is dedicated to Billy Bigelow, Anna and The King and – most of all – to the writers of the true gospels …Rodgers and Hammerstein. It's called "Wake Me Up When"'

Wake Me Up When

https://badpeoplethemusical.bandcamp.com/track/wake-me-up-when

I was dreaming of those old records that you used to play
Like Carousel and Brigadoon and Russ Conway
Dansette discs rolling round at 33 and a third
The worst record player – but the best music I ever heard

I was a kid in bed with an empty head and I loved all those sounds
Pianos ringing and the angels singing all around
It's a thousand years later but I can still remember most of the words
The worst record player – best music I ever heard

Wake me up when that time comes round again or your ghost
is walking
I'm gonna buy a cheap hi-fi and leave it on every evening
And when it's late hope to wake – to that music playing
Like Brigadoon – those old tunes take me back to you
I don't care how loud or how many people we disturb
With the worst record player – best music I ever heard

Lucy enjoys putting the song over and playing a little more energetically. She stifles a giggle as English Bob drops in some cool moves around the stage behind her. He obviously likes the song and Lucy likes his noodling. Nick Lucas seems to talk to his old Yamaha Tenor. As he blows English Bob thinks how his old Yamaha Tenor has been with him all these years. He'd sell his Mustang and his Fat Boy before he'd ever sell his YTS32.

The song even goes reasonably well with the audience and they get sporadic applause. EB and Lucy take a bow and they return to their table.

She chats to Bob afterwards as Boris, Wangly and Adrian have now moved on to discussing the finer details of Heaviside's contributions to electromagnetic theories. It all passes way over Lucy's head now.

'I do realise they don't normally listen to me Lucy. I have really enjoyed playing these songs with you!'

'Thanks Bob – it's mutual. I always thought sax goes well with acoustic songs.'

Bob pauses

'Lucy, I'm a worrier and I suspect you really do have things in life you'd like to go back and correct?'

She doesn't reply and Bob carries on.

'I wouldn't really bank on Boris completing his time machine.'

Lucy smiles and Bob continues.

'But you can depend on me.'

'I know I can Bob. Really! I'm so glad I stopped off in Lincoln City.'

After goodbyes and hugs they drive back north in a happy silence. Lucy is a little nervous that English Bob has had a few drinks but she dispels the thoughts on the grounds that she has broken so many laws recently she can't criticise anyone else. English Bob would probably get a commendation for killing Lucy; even a reward. The Manchester Bounty Hunter; doesn't bother bringing them in alive, it's too much trouble. As it turns out though, the roads are quiet and EB seems in control. Eventually, Bob pulls into the motel car park as Lucy tells him she is going to head south to San Francisco tomorrow. Bob gives her detailed directions of how to get to Marv's Motors. He makes sure she has his number too. Lucy kisses him on the cheek, climbs out of the passenger seat and carefully retrieves Nick Lucas from the rear. As Bob starts the Mustang again he leans his head out of the driver window,

'Marv's Motors – Keeps America Rolling'

Lucy responds,

'English Bob – Keeps America Rockin!'

Marv's Motors

Lucy is up early next morning, nervous about the forthcoming drive to San Francisco. She has decided to get there and lose herself in the city as soon as possible. Nice as the Oregon coast is, she has spent long enough there and needs to say goodbye to The Dog. She heads south on Highway 101. English Bob's instructions for finding Marv's Motors sound easy enough but it is a long time since she has driven in a city. Portland in the dead of night was scary enough.

> 'Follow Highway 101. South then straight over The Golden Gate. Then follow 101 through the city. Richardson Avenue, Van Ness Avenue. After crossing Market Street take the elevated 101 for 3 or 4 miles and come off east on Cesar Chavez. Under the Interstate and 5 blocks on the left. Left into Illinois Street and find Marv's Motors on the left.'

She reads English Bob's directions to herself until she has them memorised like a song lyric. Even so, she keeps the printed instructions on the seat next to her as she gets close to San Francisco. Reaching The Golden Gate Bridge she pulls off into the visitor area to gather herself. It's a bright day and she sees the city laid out before her to the left of the bridge. White clouds drift in across the bridge as container ships and sight-seeing tourist boats pass under. The sun hovers over the city. She sees Alcatraz Island in the middle of the bay and a shiver of guilt runs through her. She blocks it from her mind. She sees the traffic flowing over the bridge like corpuscular blood; the lifeblood of the city. 'Please no police! I've gotten this far.' She readies herself, starts The Dog and sets off across the bridge into the city. To her surprise it all goes as planned and she blows English Bob a kiss out of her open driver's window as she eventually leaves 101 and heads east on Cesar Chavez. It's a slightly menacing area as she finds Illinois Street and turns left into it. She slowly cruises up the street until she sees the 'Marv's Motors' sign.

A few Harleys are parked outside and she sits and observes for a while thinking things through. She reminds herself that she does have to say goodbye to The Dog or it might be a trail leading any pursuers to her. Eventually she takes a deep breath for fortitude and drives slowly into the Marv's Motors yard. She picks up her trusty rucksack and Nick Lucas and steps out of The Dog. A group of menacing looking guys are stood looking at a Harley. They see her and all stare in silence. Lucy walks slowly up to them thinking, 'I must be getting quite confident in my old age.'

The guys are text book angels. Biker boots, levis, some in worn leather jackets, oil stained and ripped T-shirts. Some are older some younger. One of the older ones deems himself the spokesperson and walks across towards her,

'Well hello young lady …You like to riiiiiiiide?'

She thinks to herself, 'If one more person calls me "young lady" I'll get my gun out and start shooting!'

She keeps her annoyance under control.

'Is Marv around?'

'Who wants to know?'

'I'm Lucy, I think he's expecting me?'

'Well we don't generally do appointments around here, but I'll take you to him.'

As they cross the yard the Angel ventures, 'I'm Don Estrada. Marv mentioned you might be arriving. You're a friend of English Bob?'

'I am indeed.'

'Well we don't do business like Ford Motors', he then effects a strange version of an English accent, 'but we do like English Bob. Airhairlair, how are you?'

Lucy finds herself laughing. They pass into a workshop area. An angel looks up from a heavy slow moving mechanical hacksaw machine. As Lucy looks down she notices a shotgun is clamped into it with the barrel being shortened. The angel looks at Don,

'This motherfucker is fuckin takin for fuckin ever Don!'

'Language Al – we have a customer!'

Don Estrada seems to command some authority and the angel stares at Lucy in bewildered silence. Don looks at the work in progress,

'That's ordnance grade steel Al. You can't rush it.'

Al nods and moves back to observing the machine aggressively. As they walk on Don mutters, 'Kids!'

Don opens a half-glazed door and leads the way into some kind of office. He bangs on a door to an adjoining room and shouts, 'Marv!!!!'

There is a sound of someone moving around and presently the door opens. Marv appears. His presence strangely dominates the room. He's aged in tight leather jeans (Lucy wonders if he slept in them) and a sleeveless denim shirt not yet buttoned up. Marv looks old but tough as the quality leather of his trousers. He walks slowly over to a coffee machine and asks, 'Anybody want a coffee?'

Lucy gratefully accepts. She realises she is still tense from the drive across SF.

Marv puts her coffee unceremoniously on the table next to where she sits. He sits opposite and pulls on his biker boots,

'Lucy is it? English Bob says I can trust you?'

'He says I can trust you too?', Lucy smiles

'That's the trust department sorted then!'

Lucy laughs and Marv continues,

'Long time since English Bob was down here, is he ok?'

'He seems fine, yeh.'

'Bob has been a good customer and helped us with a few metal working problems. He's a good guy.'

'He helped me too.'

'He says you need to lose your Dodge truck?'

'I do yes.'

'Is it yours?'

'Kind of – but I need rid now.'

'No paperwork?'

'No.'

'Where have you come from?'

'Montana.'

'Well, it's a miracle you got here without heat on you.'

'I look honest but I'm a fierce killer with eyes like fire!'

Marv laughs but then stops and stares at Lucy for a few seconds. He continues,

'I don't need to know your business Miss Lucy. I'll give you a fair price for the truck.'

Lucy is hesitant, 'It needs its identity changing because people may be looking for it?'

'We have the technology!'

'I'm serious Mr Marv. There could be nasty people looking for it.'

'Do we look like we scare easy?'

'Well no', she laughs, 'but I wouldn't want anyone getting hurt.'

'OK Lucy, we'll take that into account in the price and – thanks for the warning.'

Marv stands and shakes her hand.

'What brings you to SF anyway?'

'I need a new life and I'm into music.'

'That's a tough business. Especially in this city.'

'I know. I've been through it all elsewhere. One dead end after another.'

'Me too. Not many better buzzes than fronting a band!', he pauses, 'but hard to make a decent living?'

'I'm happy to lay low for a while until I find my way about.'

Marv looks at her, 'You got somewhere to stay?'

'I figured I'd find a hotel until I get to know my way around.'

Marv looks over at Don, 'Is Ronee still in that big house in Haight?'

'She sure is Marv.'

'She still with that Bassman who plays in Mike Remo's band?'

'Not sure Marv. I had to give him a talking to after he upset her. I let him live though!'

Marv laughs, 'Musicians eh?' Don nods.

Marv asks Lucy for the keys to The Dog so he can look it over. As he exits Don Estrada seems to look Lucy up and down. Lucy feels his piercing eyes scanning her. Eventually he speaks,

'Ronee has a big house across town and a lot of her friends are musos. I know because we've done work on one their bandvans. She's a real nice girl and her ex-boyfriend plays the bass.'

Lucy senses a serious tone in Don as he continues,

'He's harmless enough. For a musician anyway!'

Don seems to be half talking to himself now, 'They call him Thunderman. He's a good player but never makes much money. Music is a hard business. Late hours, tours, distractions.'

Lucy wonders who Ronee is and why Don is thinking out loud

for her. As Marv returns he and Don walk over to the corner of the office and look out into the yard where The Dog is parked. Lucy cant hear their discussions. Eventually Marv then walks over to a safe and opens it.

'$1400 cash Lucy? The truck, this deal and this conversation never happened?'

Lucy stands and they shake hands. She repeats her warning, 'Mr Marv, the people who may be looking for the truck are bad people.'

Marv smiles, 'You know where you stand with Bad People Lucy!'

As part of the deal Don offers to drive Lucy over to Haight Ashbury and introduce her to Ronee who might have a room to let in a house. Lucy clears everything out of The Dog and says a fond farewell and thank you, patting him on the bonnet. On the drive over town Don explains how Marv used to front a band in 'bygone years' but found he could make more money looking after people's transportation needs. He had a speciality in touring buses for the many bands out of Haight around that time. He tells her that he is part of 'what's left of The Oakland Chapter' and how Marv's place is their base this side of the Bay. He tells her about Ronee and her ex, seeming to forget his previous ramblings,

'A bass playing dude. Goes under the name of Thunderman. I think he's a good guy, he has to be because anyone hurting Ronee is dead meat!'

Lucy doesn't doubt the validity of this statement from the tone in his voice. She senses Don is fond of Ronee as Don keeps talking,

'He plays in some band called The Lowdown Dirtkickers. Marv sold them a van a few years back. Marv and their front man Mike Remo go way back.'

Lucy makes mental notes as best she can of all the names and connections. She is already excited by San Francisco and this introduction to the city. This is a bonus. She wonders how much English Bob has told them about her? She giggles to herself thinking, 'Ronee has a Guardian Angel!'

'My advice to you young lady. Don't get involved with no musicians!', Don pauses and adds 'but then, I would never take my advice either!'

They smile and laugh.

As they arrive at a house in a nice quiet residential street in

Haight Don gets out and knocks the door. A woman of similar age to Lucy answers and gives him a hug. It seems incongruous to Lucy that a young and fashionably dressed girl hugs a full on 'angel'. Lucy gets introduced and immediately gets along with Ronee. It turns out that the previous girl in the small house had skipped and not paid the last 3 months rent. Lucy is more than glad to now take the spare room in the house at a very reasonable rent. The house is in need of considerable repair but Lucy immediately begins to feel at home. She moves her belongings into her room (which doesn't take long) and then helps Ronee assemble a flatpack table for the kitchen. Lucy enjoys the methodical task and slows down Ronee's impetuous nature. They both stand back and admire the results when the table is complete. Lucy offers to walk around to the Chinese store around the corner and cook an inaugural meal for the table. She loses herself in thoughts of what to prepare.

*

As she lies in bed that night Lucy has a glimpse of some kind of contentment. So much so that she becomes nervous of it all being fucked up up by unresolved circumstance. She thanks her lucky stars for the breaks she's had. She now realises how easy it would have been for her to be stopped by highway patrol and then she'd have been dead in the water. She trembles at the thought, realising she has been running on adrenalin and not thinking straight for days or was it weeks? The Snakes slither into her mind and she shivers. She banishes them and decides she has a chance here and that she will lay low and just survive for as long as it takes. She has no idea how long that will be. She lies in bed and listens to the distant sounds of the city.

*

Ronee has just landed a new job as a legal clerk and is off to work early the next day. True to her word though, she has left a list of bars and cafes that hire and pay fairly. Lucy walks into Haight and soon finds herself in casual work. No records and cash in hand. Lucy doesn't see too much of Ronee as she falls into a routine of bar work but whenever they are in the house together she and Ronee get along well. On Lucy's first night off from the bar Ronee insists they go down to a local bar for a beer. Ronee is inquisitive,

'How the hell did you meet Don and Marv?'

'A friend in Oregon recommended them.'

Ronee laughs, 'Recommended The Gruesome Twosome?'

'Well, I was told Marv would take a truck off my hands for cash.'

'Marv would take your hand off for cash!'

'They seem ok to me?'

'Well, as Bad People go they are ok', she pauses, 'I suppose.'

'You don't sound convinced?'

'My Mum once attacked Don with an axe.'

'Woh?'

Ronee stares into space, 'That was just before she moved to LA with her boyfriend.'

'How come you didn't go?'

'I didn't like her boyfriend.'

'How come she didn't end up in jail?'

'Don wouldn't press charges. He always says it would be embarrassing for an angel to resort to the law.'

'He seems fond of you?'

'Well he rents me the house.'

Lucy decides not to seem to pry and instead Lucy recounts a heavily censored version of how she travelled down in The Dog from Montana.

'What did you do in Montana?'

'I lived with my boyfriend.'

'You split?'

'Well – yes. He turned into a complete shitwit!'

'What did he do?'

'He was a musician. That's how we met.'

'I used to go with a bass player. He is ok really but spends a long time going nowhere. He's happy, as long as he has a drink in his hand and somewhere to sleep.'

Lucy is reminded of English Bob's story of work in a steel plant and how it was really a jail sentence.

'Lot to be said for that Ronee. No-one has control over you. If you're gonna work may as well work for yourself?'

'I guess.'

Ronee returns from the bar with two more beers.

'So you left him and used his truck as a getaway vehicle?'

Lucy smiles, 'I guess', she pauses before continuing, 'I'd decided to leave anyways and I think he'd realised.'

Ronee notices as Lucy nervously clasps her hands; knuckles white. The beer fuels Lucy's mouth now,

'His family were scary. Really scary. I mean fucking scary. I know Seth was scared of them too. He told me when we first met. Seth was a crazy good musician and his father ran a band. A good band too if you like real lowdown threatening blues. I went to a couple of gigs soon after Seth and I ended up in Montana. We'd tried to build a following as a duo but it didn't work out. Out of the blue Seth told me he owned a farm; or at least his father had put one in his name.'

Lucy rambles, 'Oh shit the gigs were scary. Low lifes know how to party. I'm pretty sure his father dealt drugs. Seth did introduce me one time but his father and brother just ignored me. I don't even know if Seth told them much about me. Keerrrrrissst Ronee his Dad was so so scary. His brothers too.'

She takes a mouthful of her beer and giggles, 'Their surname was Snake and the band was called The Snake Brothers or sometimes Snakemen!' Lucy adopts a hiss as she speaks of them.

Ronee listens intently. Lucy sees she has Ronee spellbound.

'Funny thing is they actually look like snakes!'

Ronee splutters her beer laughing, 'Fuck off! You were with a snake? Did he have a snake in his trousers?'

Lucy laughs too, 'It's true (pause) but Seth was a good looking snake.'

'Was?!', Ronee asks, feigning seriousness.

Lucy realises her slip and quickly adds, 'Well …I mean he was a lot better looking before he started back in the family band full time. They drank a lot. He used to come back from gigs in vicious moods and always looked older somehow.'

Ronee looks puzzled, not quite believing as Lucy carries on providing information, more to cover her conversation tracks than anything else.

'There is a sister too and she plays bass in the band but she doesn't look like the men. She is slinky but in a different kind of way. I could never get Seth to talk about her really.'

Ronee interrupts, 'Won't he be after you to get his truck back?'

'Noooooo – I don,t think he'll be too bothered.'

'LuLu, you are so naïve! They always want their trucks back.'

Lucy suddenly looks worried and Ronee notices. A tear descends from her left eye. Ronee reaches over the table and puts her hand on Lucy's. Lucy looks at Ronee, tearful now, 'They might come for me.'

Ronee tries to backtrack, 'Hey, don't worry it's only a truck and it would be a long way to come. Would they know where to find you anyway?'

Lucy trembles, 'No – but we were married.'

'She-ite Lucy – you never told me that! You WERE married? Did you D-I-V-O-R-C-E?'

'No.'

'So you are still married?'

'No – well – yes', Lucy is panicking.

Ronee calms her down slowly. Eventually Lucy explains how they tried to get married in Vegas once but Seth had no official papers so they couldn't but a couple of weeks later he said he had arranged it all in Reno. It was very rushed but Seth had been keen to do it that way. She never wanted to cause her family the expense of a wedding or anything and it seemed romantic at the time. She looks so lost as Ronee listens. Ronee holds her hands tight.

'Look LuLu. If you were married then sooner or later you will need to get it annulled. That's not like divorce because it means you got married under false circumstances. Like maybe he never told you he had a criminal record? It could even be that you weren't ever properly married? Sounds to me like that could be the case?'

Lucy frantically pulls her thoughts together, 'I can't let them know where I am?'

Ronee calms her down slowly, 'Hey leave it with me LuLu. Let me check if you are actually married. If not you are in the clear? If you are we'll have to work out an annulment somehow? There will be a way.'

Lucy trembles now as she speaks, 'They must never know where I am?'

Ronee realises how desperate Lucy is comforts her now.

'Leave it with me LuLu. First we box off the problem and then we find the best way to solve it!'

Lucy nods in agreement.

*

A couple of weeks pass slowly for Lucy. She changes her hair colour and style. Ronee compliments her but understands the real reason. One evening before leaving for the work Lucy prepares a meal for her and Ronee. Ronee asks,

'Hey LuLu – your ex was called Seth Snake – right?'

Lucy looks up in concern, 'Yes?'

'And you said you were married in Reno?'

'Yes?'

'Well – I checked the marriage registers in Nevada and Montana!'

'Yes?'

'And there is no mention of any Seth Snake or Lucy Snake nee Smith!'

'So that means I was never married?'

'That's right The Mascara Snake!'

Lucy laughs at the Captain Beefheart reference but inwardly a load lifts from her mind. Ronee continues, 'I also checked records in Montana and there are no records of any Seth Snake. So, even if you had been officially married it would be a void marriage. That would be an easy process.'

'You're the top lawyer in the whole universe Ronee!'

Ronee smiles and stands with hands on hips, 'I rest my case!', and adds for good measure, 'It would be my contention that the lowdown sonoffabitch piece of shit just wanted you to think you were married?'

Lucy nods and lets out a long sigh, 'Fuuuuuuurrrrrrrckkkkkkk! How dumb am I?'

'So, MISS LuLu Smith I think it's about time you got yourself out and about a bit more and got back into the singing? I've heard you singing and it's good.'

'Maybe I should?'

'No maybe about it. I'll get in touch with my old boyfriend Thunderman. He can give us the buzz on the best places to play?'

Lucy thinks carefully. Although she has studiously kept low for what must be 6 months now she has begun to get used to life in SF and weighs that she does need to circulate a little more.

'Thanks Ronee, I'd appreciate that. I appreciate it all. I OWE you big time.'

*

Lucy is in sleepless-night-city. Part of her feels happier; much happier. Part of her feels bad for not having told Ronee the full story; but then, how could she? Ronee is right she IS/WAS totally naïve and she should've realised the marriage was fake. Seth was a FakeSnake. They are all FakeSnakes. She wonders how that changes things? She thinks back. Jake Snake never spoke to her and neither did the rest of the family. They never visited the farm for the two years she was there with Seth. She should've just left instead of waiting to explain it was over. How naïve was she? On a scale of naivety from 1 to 10 she was FUCKING naïve! She figures that with any luck The Snakes won't know anything about her; apart from what Seth told them. What could he tell them? She told him she came from a town overlooking Lake Michigan. She told him her Dad had a qualification in Physics. He knew her surname Smith; so what the fuck; wasn't it the most common name in the world. Her biggest fear was a photograph. If the Snakes involved the police they could put out the proverbial 'APB'. She hoped that The Snakes were as bad as she suspected and they would never go to 'the law'; but, on the other hand they would be looking for her. She reasoned that Mrs Snake would be distraught; course she would, she'd lost a son; shot twice and burnt to a crisp. Oh fuck! How bad was she? As she finally drifted off into a snake infested swamp-sleep, surrounded by rank mist and the sound of gators sliding from muddy river banks into dirty water her last logical thought was – that – with any luck – the state police or FBI wouldn't be involved – the disappearance of Seth Snake would not be reported – The Snakes would be looking as far as they could cast their web (wasn't that spiders?) but they wouldn't EVER find her. Maybe she'd ask Ronee about the mechanics of changing your name? What about The Dog though? Could they ever trace it? She'd taken every precaution? She figured Marv to unload it anonymously. She'd been running, running, running. Running on adrenalin and taking respite in short bursts wherever and whenever. She had nightmare thoughts of The Snakes slithering out of Montana, interrogating Howard and Elizabeth, slithering through Seattle through shit filled sewers and under dead of night, torturing English Bob before sliding noiselessly into the Bay at Sausalito heading for San Francisco. She wakes in a cold cold cold sweat.

It was good news followed by a bad night. She opens the curtains to a nondescript grey day and for some reason she feels better. Much better. Perhaps she has a chance after all? For the first time in weeks she takes Nick Lucas from his case and wonders where her song notebook is. She has to delve deep into her rucksack for it where it is still packed under the box containing Howard's gun. She is shocked by the weight of the package. She puts the package on the bed next to her and, as she does, she thinks of Howard and Elizabeth. Then she looks at her song notebook and the idea to make up a song about the gun appears. She opens the package and stares at the weapon. She shivers. She wonders if she could use it on Jake Snake if he walked in now. She's done it before, she could do it again? She looks at Nick Lucas and thinks, 'the things I do for you!' She shivers and wishes Ronee was home. The gun becomes her and Nick Lucas' friend and she begins to string chords together and scribble in the book. She has no idea how much time has passed but now she stares down at a set of words with very few corrections. She plays it through a few times?

Waiting

https://badpeoplethemusical.bandcamp.com/track/waiting

There'll be a time when you need me
When burglars invade
There'll be a time you want me
When you're consumed with rage
And you'll need more of me
When you got a war to wage
You all love my simplicity
The whole world is my stage

Until then I'm just waiting
That's what I do
It's not frustrating
Patience is my virtue

You know where I am
You know what I do
No evil in me – is it with you
My aim is true
My aim is up to you

You've loved me for centuries
No need to be scared
I'm company for sentries
Stop who goes there?
You need more than muscle
When your arms are bare
With me in your pocket
You are safe everywhere

Give me ammunition
It's your decision

I offer protection
From all insurrection
Life is safer – for both of us
Pull the trigger feel the buzz
My aim is true
My aim is up to you

If you desire – I can be vicious
There was a liar – said life is precious

I never make mistakes
And I do as I'm told
If you don't like someone
I can stop them getting old

A few days later finds Ronee and Lucy walking down Columbus Avenue and entering an open mic bar. Ronee introduces 'Thunderman' to Lucy. Thunderman is friendly but immediately concerned with rekindling things with Ronee. Lucy likes Thunderman though and she giggles to herself as she thinks of Don Estrada giving him a 'talking to'. Thunderman buys them both a beer as Lucy sits nervously waiting for a chance to play.

The compere guy in charge pays no attention until Ronee asks TMan to go across and fix it with him. On Thunderman's intervention the compere looks over to Lucy and nods. Lucy nervously takes the stage and quickly takes out Nick Lucas. She's all clumsy fingers and klutzy thumbs as she tries to get settled. The compere seems impatient and the sound man is less than attentive. The compere asks her name and, not wanting to use her real name, she goes with Ronee's nickname for her. He asks where she's from and she replies 'Illinois.'

'Ladies and gents, a big welcome to LuLu from Illinois.' There's an unenthusiastic round of applause.

She plays her Highway 99 song, figuring that it went down ok in Lincoln City with English Bob on saxophone. However, she is nervous and this audience is bigger and a lot tougher. The sound is not right.

She checks the tuning of Nick Lucas and struggles with nervousness finding herself talking a little too much as she struggles with tuning and tries to think of what to play next and finds herself burbling about her saxophone player not being here. She is suddenly aware of a 'presence' on stage next to her. She thinks she's been bumped but the presence introduces himself as Mike Remo and unpacks a saxophone,

'I'll play some saxophone for you?'

He smiles. Lucy remembers her song 'Gravity' and tells Mike the key. Mike smiles and encouragingly pats her shoulder. I like your voice LuLu. Mike takes the mic for a second,

'What do you call 500 soundmen at the bottom of the ocean?'

The audience fall silent, Mike is quite obviously a 'presence' in the whole club. No-one offers any answers so Mike answers his own question,

'A good start!'

The sound man looks up from a girl he is talking to; Mike stares over at him, 'I'm sure the sound is good here though?'

The sound man looks down at his mixing desk in full concentration now.

Lucy starts the song and she hears the adjustments kick in. Nick Lucas sounds way way better and her voice projects. Mike Remo smiles over at her and it gives her confidence.

Gravity

https://badpeoplethemusical.bandcamp.com/track/gravity

There must be some kind mathematical beauty
A brutal empire can't crush
Some kind of unification theory
Space and time is twisted enough
All the planets spin around
We are prisoners of the ground
Gravity drags us all down

We got tablets of stone
And we got rulers sittin on thrones
But the Queen dropped her crown
It's broken on the ground
Gravity drags us all down

Birds might fly
High in the sky
But everything falls
Nobody knows why

I don't need St Teresa's heart in a glass
I got a lover's heart to trespass
I watch every flake of snow
Settle on the cold ground below
Gravity drags us down don't you know

Mike doesn't add anything until the end of the song (unlike many saxophone players) and he's happy to just look cool. He's mastered cool. He tags on a really nice break at the end. Mike obviously commands a presence as the audience fall silent and this time there is applause. Good applause.

Lucy packs Nick away and thanks Mike for his help. He smiles back, 'No, thank you that's a beauty little song. Let's collect our free beers for playing?'

Lucy smiles 'of course.' Soon they are at the bar each with an IPA in hand. Lucy remembers Mike's name from her chat with Don Estrada the Angel.

'Are you a friend of Marv?'

Mike looks over to her with surprise, 'Marv's Motors: Keeps America Rolling?'

'That's the one.'

'There's only one Marv! Me and him go way back.'

Ronee comes over and joins them. She jumps up and down in excitement, 'Hey LuLu – really good!'

She nods to Mike, 'Mike Remo; Mister Skulk-Rock; still blowing hard I see?'

'Always Ronee. How is my old friend Don Estrada?'

'He's good Mike.'

'He once threatened to kill me!'

'Well you're still alive so he can't've meant it?'

Mike smiles knowingly at Ronee. 'He's the badassest of Bad People everywhere Ronee!'

6

Party Like A Demon

Weeks pass. Lucy slips into a routine of sorts. She now has two casual bar jobs and just manages to pay the rent Ronee charges and put a bit to the side. She grows to love Ronee like the sister she never had even though they don't see so much of each other. Ronee's job is going well and she seems to love the work whereas Lucy is usually working afternoons or evenings and nights now. Whenever they can they share cooking duties. As the winter slowly passes Lucy finds time to get out to a few more open mic nights and, as spring brings fluffy white clouds to the city, she even gets offered gigs at a few folky bars. Ronee has an 'on/off' time with Thunderman; Lucy likes him even though Ronee is wary of musicians.

'Hey Lulu, you should get out to more gigs?'

Lucy smiles at Ronee, 'I still need to keep a low profile for a while Ron. If I make *The Late Show* The Snakes might see it!'

'Do they have TV in Montana?'

'Unfortunately, yes!'

'Well Mike Remo's band is playing in Castro this weekend. Thunderman wants me to go? I don't fancy hanging without a friend while he's onstage.'

Lucy finds herself smiling at the thought but reminds herself that she really ought to lay low. In the back of her mind she has The Snakes and she knows she can't get lower than The Snakes, no matter how low. Always present, always a worry. The Fucking Snakes.

Lucy snaps out of her daynightmares as Ronee continues, 'Mike Remo is a good contact and he seems to like you and your songs?'

Lucy smiles at Ronee, knowing how much she owes her, 'Ok, let's go. I need a night out for sure.'

Something in Lucy's mind still tells her to 'keep low' but her lonely life of recent weeks needs alleviation. Anyways, she always enjoys Ronee's company.

'Sounds great Ronee!'

It's after dark when they set out. Lucy feels suitably inconspicuous as they walk through Haight towards Castro. As they approach the venue Lucy becomes aware of a tension. She can't work out why. On entering the venue a guy who knows Ronee smiles and let's them in for free. Lucy becomes even more tense as the crowd seem to be wired. Not dissimilar to the peoples who generally attended Snake Brothers gigs; maybe that was it? It burrows into her mind. She feels nervous electricity run along her spine and into her hair. She mentally tries to shrink herself and moves to the side of the room standing by a pillar. Ronee looks concerned and gets them both a couple of beers.

'You ok Lulu?'

Lucy nods nervously looking around her. She thinks out loud, 'This reminds me of SnakeGigs.'

'Nah, these are The Dirtkickers. They are nice guys really. They got this idea of Skulk Rock but it's just a front; personalities they like to hide behind. Anyway, you met Mike Remo and Thunderman. They are nice guys?'

Lucy looks downwards, slightly tense, but Ronee clinks her beer bottle against Lucy's and smiles,

'The band sometimes attract the old "angels" crowd and consequently try and appear mean and lowdown, like their name, but they're harmless. Let's have a beer and forget the world outside?'

Lucy nods and tries to smile.

Mike Remo and The Lowdown Dirtkickers take the stage. It takes them a while to get the audience onside but eventually the atmosphere becomes more exuberant and a better humour seems to pervade the venue. Mike Remo works the audience. Mike can handle any kind of hecklers it would seem. Lucy looks around. Suspicious characters abound and some stare at her and Ronee. As a few menacing guys move closer, Lucy is on the point of walking out until Don Estrada appears from nowhere. He hugs Ronee and smiles at Lucy, shaking her hand. The menacing guys now retreat; they are lightweight against the presence of Don. The audience suddenly erupt as Mike Remo announces one particular song, 'Party hard and party long, you're not round for very long, we're all bad people, worship at the crooked steeple, party like a fuckin demon!'

Party Like A Demon

https://badpeoplethemusical.bandcamp.com/track/party-like-a-demon

Well give me the music
Keep the groove and don't lose it
One minute you're here and then you're gone
So party like a demon all night long

My Daddy said 'Son, you're going wrong
You fly too close to the sun
You fly too high and too long
When you fall you will be gone'

So – **party like a demon**
Party like a demon all night long
Party like a demon til you're gone

I don't got much to take pride in
But prides no good when you're gone
I'm slippin and slidin'
Into hell and beyond

Party Like A Demon

And will you pass me the whore?
I wanna party some more
Pass me over the Merck
I don't want to go to work
I got the devil right by my side
Told the sonoffabitch – get a life

They call me Mr Six Gun
I'm loaded all night long
I party like a demon til you're gone

Party like a demon
Your life is a wound and it's bleedin
So party like a demon
All night long

As the song progresses it seems to encourage worse and worse behaviour from the audience. At first it's funny but then turns darker. People always pushing at boundaries and the boundaries seem to give way easily here. Bad behaviour and unlikeable characters begin to rule the night. Bad People.

Lucy looks more and more ill at ease. She whispers to Ronee and begins to edge her way towards the exit. As she moves through the crowd she looks back at the band and seems to catch the guitar players eye. He looks kind of out of place; a little like she feels. As she makes it to the exit she hears the song end and the audience hooting. 'Fucking stoners!'

She finds a railing and leans on it catching the twinkle of the spring stars. She thinks of her father and his amateur cosmology. Maybe Boris The Cranium is right and gravity is electromagnetic in nature? She thinks her Dad would get on well with him. She wonders how English Bob is these days. Anything to take her mind off snake-behaviour.

A strange accent shocks her out of her thoughts.

'Hello. Starry night?'

She turns to see the guitar player from the band leaning on the railing too with a bottle of beer. His opening line dazes her as she inwardly panics thinking he might be from Montana. She gathers and looks him over, trying to look unapproachable but he continues,

'Are you a friend of Mike Remo's?'

'Well, he helped me out with a song once.'

'That's it. You sang with him in a bar downtown before Christmas. I knew I remembered you.'

Lucy thinks, 'fuck, fuck, fuck, so much for keeping a low profile.'

'I'm James. You are good. Been working much?'

'Too much.'

'Speak to Mike he knows where all the good gigs are.'

'Oh not in music. I have some bar jobs.'

'That's a waste.'

'Where are you from?'

'Manchester England.'

She looks him over again

'You know Morrissey?'

'I wish.'

'Me too', she finds herself smiling until she remembers the last song.

'Are all your numbers like that?'

'No, but that one always goes well; The Devil's Music you know?'

'He can keep it!'

James tries to laugh,

'Hey, you should hear some of our other songs?'

Lucy looks scornful

'I've had a bellyful of songs like that. My ex used to play in a band that majored in it!'

'A San Francisco Band?'

'No, was up in' (she pauses) 'errrrm Idaho.'

'Wow, you're a long way from home.'

'This is home now, was hoping it would be an improvement.'

'I'm sure it will be. So your ex is definitely your ex?'

'Oh yes, I finally managed to convince him of that!'

Lucy begins to move away. James places a nervous hand on her shoulder, she brushes it away.

'Come see us again, we have nicer songs that I made up?'

As she turns the corner of the building she looks back. James is still looking at her and smiling. She finds herself smiling back before walking off at speed. She mutters to herself 'Party like a FUCKING demon.' Then an afterthought, 'nice accent though!'

7

The Saloon

James sits alongside Thunderman in The Dirtkicker's van as they sit in the early evening traffic on Columbus Avenue. James drums on the dashboard,

'Three sets tonight TMan?'

'It will be.'

'We never make so much money though?'

'I know but Mike likes to do this gig. Him and the manageress go way back.'

'She let's us charge five bucks entry. All the dumb limey tourists love it. They wanna hear "The Blues" man!'

'And we give them Skulk Rock?'

'Indeed we do Jimmy English. We need to educate them.'

'Skulk Rock is the way forward TMan. Just that the world don't quite know it quite yet.'

'But they will!'

'That's right The Mascara Snake.'

'Fast and Boolbous.'

'Bulbous also tapered?'

'Yeh but you gotta wait until I say – also a tin teardrop.'

They collapse into laughter. TMan asks, 'You're in a fine mood Jimmy E, not in love AGAIN are you?'

James laughs and does not answer as he continues drumming on the dash. His thoughts elsewhere. TMan stares at him momentarily, smiling.

They arrive at the venue and unload the equipment. There is a house PA and drum kit that The MetroGnome is happy to use; he presently arrives with Mike Remo and his cymbals. Mike chats with the manageress as the 3 Dirtkickers check the setup and sound.

The Dirtkickers sit and chat as they wait for the venue to fill up. James looks anxiously at the people entering by the door at the far end of the bar. Thunderman notices and asks,

'Expecting someone Jimmy English?'

TMan looks at The MetroGnome and they smile.

'Wouldn't be the Susanville Siren by any chance?'

'The Supermodel Lady?'

Then they sing 'She's a power dresser – A Harley won't impress her.'

The Gnome slaps his thigh and carries on 'Legs so long and heels so high – you need a pilot's licence to look her in the eye!!!'

They roll about laughing as James glares at them.

They're still laughing as Mike Remo sits next to them. TMan splutters through laughter,

'Jimmy English is still lovesick Mike!'

'Not the woman who put the Susan in Susanville is it? That was months ago?'

James reddens up as Mike sings,

'I'm ready for you – but there's no you – I feel so low when you don't show – so so so sad and blue.'

He yodels the last line and TMan and The Gnome roll about laughing.

James looks at them and splutters, 'fuck off you shitheaded pieces of shit!'

The 3 of them turn silent – staring at him – before laughing even more voluminously. Mike Remo calls over to the bar

'Four beers please Marg – we got a lervsick geetar player!'

They all smile.

*

As their beers are finished they take the stage. The first set goes well with the crowd composed of some regulars and some tourists. Marg never rips off the tourists and the Europeans find the beer prices attractive. At the end of the first set the band sit in a corner, some people leave others stay on. One English guy is complimentary and pleased to find out Jimmy English is from Manchester. The conversation makes James think of home.

They sit around for another 30 minutes before Mike Remo decides to start the 2nd set. As they play a new clientele wander in. This time they get a few dancers one of whom is extremely attractive. James watches her entice a succession of shy and not so shy men onto the dance floor. Mike Remo walks over to James during a drum and bass breakdown and says, 'We should have her at every gig. Dancers are always welcome.' He adds, 'Don't go falling in love again Jimmy English!', with an evil grin. The 2nd set ends and The Saloon is now filled to capacity. The gig is going well and The Dirtkickers take the stage for the final set. The attractive dancer works her magic and there is plenty of gyration on the dance floor. As the set progresses James again finds himself scanning the audience for Felicia. The 'advice' of Mike Remo, Thunderman and The Gnome bounce around in his head and he tries to forget her. The set goes really well as they get to the last of 3 encores. Mike Remo announces it,

'Thanks for skulk rockin in San Francisco – here's a song about living for the moment so – please – get another beer and – see y'all next time!'

Nothing Outside of Today

https://badpeoplethemusical.bandcamp.com/track/nothing-outside-of-today

All time is trapped tonight
And we got it all
Put real life outside
Under the stars in the sky

They ain't ever gonna fade away
They ain't ever gonna fall
There's nothing outside of today
Nothing at all

This life is nothing to me
That life is like a movie
They all want to sue me
But I got nothing to fear.
The moment that you try
Is the moment you start to die
Don't ask me why
It's God's idea

Stars never fade away

They never fall
There's nothing outside of today
Nothing at all

Is there a fate
Time just delays
And we're too late
To change our ways

Throw my star into the night sky
Teach my thoughts to fly
The limitations of this life
Are in the body not the mind

Stars never fade away
They never fall
There's nothing outside of today
Nothing at all

James thinks to himself, 'Wow, this is one of our best gigs?'

He loves his guitar sound and the electricity returning from the audience. The extrovert dancer moves to a position in front of him and smiles as he rips his guitar break.

As the audience sway with the music he notices a ripple of faces turn as though a current through the crowd. Slowly the 'disturbance' moves forward past the bar area. Finally, the crowd seems to part and Felicia appears. James feels a shock of electricity. Her presence seems to alter the equilibrium of the whole room. A strange phenomenon to behold as a zone seems to establish around her. Men look but look away in case she turns them to stone. The atmosphere seems to change as the extrovert dancer no longer rules the room.

As the song ends Mike Remo thanks the audience and informs them of the next gig. James immediately leaves the stage and goes to Felicia.

'Hiya, you made it!'

'Only just, it would appear!'

'Well I'm glad you made it. Can I get you a drink?'

'A cold beer would be great.'

James gets the beers and sits with Felicia. He is nervous.

'Great to seat you. I mean see you!'

Felicia laughs confidently, 'I do so love your accent. What brings a Scotsman to San Francisco?'

'Hey – I'm English!!'

'Isn't it the same?'

'Fuck no. They are strange.'

Felicia looks puzzled.

'I'll explain on our 3rd date?' (James grows in confidence).

Felicia laughs, 'It's a deal! For our 2nd date you can take me to a party? It's up in The Heights.'

'OK. When is it?'

She laughs now, 'It's tonight!'

Mike Remo looks over at James as he packs away his saxophone. He smiles. He takes time out and walks over. He waves his finger at Felicia, 'Susanville. I never forget a face!', he looks at James, 'Jimmy English, we'll take your rig back to HQ and see you Sunday?'

James smiles at him. As Mike walks away Felicia sparkles, 'Looks like you're a free agent? 2nd date it is then?'

She tosses her head back as she smiles. The shockwave it creates ripples his thoughts. It seems to slow down time. Whiplash waves slowly traverse the length of her dark hair scattering light across her cheeks. A wayward strand crosses her forehead until her slender finger slips under it and herds it back into line.

'Well I'm not usually that easy. But if you insist?'

She stares at him for two million years but he never gets bored; never blinks. Eventually, she speaks,

'OK, let's go.'

Most things other than Felicia drain from his mind although he does excuse himself to go over and pack his guitar into its case. He smiles at TMan and The Gnome and gives them the Skulk Rock Salute. He wanders through the bar with Felicia, feeling the jealousy waves from men (they want to be with her) and women (they want to be like her) alike.

Felicia

Felicia's Porsche is parked nearby. James feels a rush of excitement as he slides into the passenger seat. Soon they are hurtling north on Columbus before Felicia hangs a sharp left and guns the Porsche up a hill east. He glances at her heels and her expert feet on the pedals. The city lights blur as they fly past. Strangely, he feels at ease with Felicia and no pressure to talk for its own sake. He looks at her hair float in the night air revealing her neck. He notices she wears no jewelry. He looks at the night sky and stars appear from behind clouds. He purposefully blinks fully expecting to wake up soon. Perhaps back in Manchester with the smell of frying bacon drifting up the stairs. He is mightily relieved when he opens his eyes to see them fly past the lower end of Lombard Street.

'Where are we going?'

'Private club in The Heights. They have a band I like and, with any luck we can get a beer and find a quiet spot to listen in peace.'

James smiles.

'I think you might like the band', she adds.

James senses Felicia really means it. He looks at her in silence as she drives confident in her decision making. They pull into a driveway and Felicia links his arm as she guides him up the street.

'Sometimes people just wind me up Jimmy and I remembered your band were playing tonight!'

'Glad you did Felicia.'

James is somehow pleased with himself for saying her name. Even more so as she smiles. He looks down the street as they walk and sees the moon over The Bay. He sees Alcatraz shimmer in moonlight,

'You escaped for a while?'

She looks at him, 'I did!'

Two security men on the door seem to know Felicia and open an inconspicuous door for her. James feels their eyes burn into him. He feels like he's been picked up on a Star Trek Tricorder. He follows Felicia down some stairs into a wide open basement and Felicia leads him to a room where music is playing. As they enter she directs James to a quiet table at the rear and goes to the bar. She returns with 2 large beers. The band are a 3 piece. Felicia seems quite excited as she tells James about them,

'They're English too.'

'What are they called?'

'Distant Meteors.'

James pauses for thought, 'wow, good name.'

Felicia giggles, 'Yes I saw them here once before. You reminded me of them.'

James enjoys the music and he enjoys watching Felicia enjoy the music. He watches her ankle flex as her foot taps. He watches her wrist flex as she drums her slender fingers on the table. His brain cells seem to soar. They follow his gaze along her slender arms. She looks at him and smiles. For some crazy reason he thinks of home. He can't work out why? Maybe he feels settled all of a sudden? He looks at the curl of her hair around her ear. He tries to slow down time. A distant dark star somehow radiates a message to him. He somehow knows these moments can't and won't last. He banishes the thoughts and his eyes follow the line of her eyebrow and down the slight curve of her nose. Strangely in keeping with his thoughts the singer of the band introduces the 'last number for tonight',

'Thanks for listening ladies and gentlemen. This one is called Time.'

Time

https://badpeoplethemusical.bandcamp.com/track/time

This is the crazy song
Because all of your love is gone
This is like a world gone wrong
This is the world where I belong
This is the world where I belong

And I'm stuck in the Starlight City
I want to fight but nobody will hit me

My girlfriend just told me
This life is so lonely
If I love you only

Time can't change me
I change time

And I'm runnin' like a Baskerville hound
Time is travelling all the way down
I'm still as fast as ultrasound
Catching up with the world spinning round
Catching up with the world just spinning around

Time can't change me
Cos I change time
Time can't change me
I change time all the time

Cold twilight all along this street
I've got shadows that begin at my feet
But I've still got my speed
I got my fog, my pearls, my amphetamine
Got my brown bag – I got my morphine

As the song finishes there is scant applause from the audience and James feels slightly self-conscious as he finds himself applauding loudly and whistling (a talent he'd always been blessed with). Felicia looks at him and smiles, unembarrassed by his appreciative response.

'I'm glad you liked the band Jimmy English!'

'I really did!!'

'People in this club are not so into music Jimmy. I sometimes feel sorry for the bands.'

'Is that why you liked us?'

'Nooo Jimmy. When I saw you I saw different audience reactions than here. That time up in Susanville the audience loved you.'

'Skulk Rock is going to take over the world! The time is nigh!'

'I hope so.'

James detects a sincerity in Felicia's statement. He is shocked by her real interest in Skulk Rock. It's a bonus. He now knows he is in love for sure. He nervously holds her hand. No negative electricity flows into him. It's a positive sign. They smile and James goes for more beers. He waits an age at the bar for an airheaded barmaid to fix some complicated cocktails for a bonedome shithead in a suit. His innerself screams, 'Fucking useless bitch. You wouldn't last five fucking minutes in The Duke of York!' He can't find it in his heart to disagree with his innerself either. The consensus set in stone as she charges him $25 for two beers. 'Fucking useless bitch!' As he returns to the table he nearly drops $25 worth of beer as he sees Felicia deep in conversation with three more jaw dropping women. Felicia looks almost apologetic as she introduces Amanda, Yolande and Miranda. He smiles at each of them as they are introduced. The girls are friendly but inevitably chat to Felicia about things they have in common. James tries his best but finds himself free-falling out of the conversation. Felicia exchanges a look with him. James contemplates suicide before excusing himself to walk over and have a word with the 3 guys in the band who are busy packing away. It turns out they are from Newcastle England and on a mini-tour of the Pacific North West. It refreshes James to chat with English guys again and as he walks back to Felicia's table he is once again thinking of his parents.

As he approaches the table he is shocked to see his seat next to Felicia taken up by a well dressed but obviously inebriated guy. The girls seem to dote on his every word as he moves ever closer to Felicia. Two other men stand in front of the table now and form some kind of physical and social barrier to him reclaiming his seat. He fails to attract Felicia's eye and retreats to the bar for another beer. Suddenly his gleaming space ship that swept past stars was grounded by a gravity it couldn't handle. He flicked through the manuals for a way to handle this situation but it is a circumstance he has never encountered before. He goes to the weapons manual and begins to read the section on multiple targets. Should he set phasors to stun or kill? He leans on the bar; suddenly an out-of-place figure amongst well dressed and confident revellers, this time hoping the 'useless bitch' keeps him waiting even longer. As his mental tricorder scans his targets Amanda peels off from the table and comes over to the bar. She stands next to James sympathetically explains,

'An unexpected guest!', she smiles at James.

'I worked that much out', he tries to smile.

'Felicia's fiancée. He was supposed to be out of town this weekend.'

James can't hide his sudden depression. Amanda sees his disappointment and carries on,

'I'm sure 'Fil' didn't expect him and I'm sure she's grateful you were discreet!', she touches the back of his hand on the bar and adds, 'I'm sure she'll be in touch.'

'Who is he?'

'Oh, that's Rich. We call him "Rich Guy" he's very very loaded.'

Amanda looks vaguely ashamed as she explains and appends, ' … .but he's ok really.'

She smiles at James in an understanding manner, 'I'm sure Fil will be in touch!', and she walks back to her table.

James draws a deep breath and curses under it. He curses again and again AND AGAIN! He exits the club and draws even deeper on the fresh night air. He walks around a corner and again sees the shimmering bay under moonlight. He is lost but knows which general direction to walk in as he sings to himself,

'When you're lost in the fucking night – In Pacific fucking Heights!'

Pacific Heights

https://badpeoplethemusical.bandcamp.com/track/pacific-heights-if-only

When you're lost in the night
In Pacific Heights
And nothing turns out right
And everything you do
Turns to the blues
And your brain just blew a fuse

When the crazy neighbourhood command
Can't understand
Why you're waiting for a new escape plan

So only the brave die slowly
So lost and so lonely

Live a life so lowly
If only, if only, if only, if only

My phasor set to kill
Death can be such a bitter pill
Tell me your last wish if you will?
In orbit round a dim star
Upholding intergalactic law
With silver spurs and a tin star

If I could fly in the sky I know I'd fall over
But if you buy me a pint then I'll buy you another
And another, and another, and another

So only the brave die slowly
So lost and so lonely
Live a life so lowly
If only, if only, if only, if only

Stealing Stars

Lucy walks through San Francisco streets between bar jobs. For the first time in weeks she feels restless. She has been Ms LowProfile for months now. The SnakeMares have faded a little and she wonders how to map the future. 'What future?', she says to herself. Seth's ghost walks into her mind and she tells it to 'Fuck Right Off.' It's a quiet night in the bar she watches a never ending baseball game on call to deliver beer to the regulars of the bar. She hears a Harley Davidson cruise past as the bar door opens and Ronee enters followed by Don Estrada, Marv (of Marv's Motors) and Mike Remo. They take a quiet table at the rear and Ronee comes over to the bar,

'Hey LuLu Mike Remo is putting together an all-dayer and he needs some performers so I brought them down here!', Ronee looks pleased with herself.

'I dunno Ronee', Lucy hesitates.

'C'mon LuLu you need to break out and make some more of your talent?'

Lucy is struck by the intent in Ronee's tone. Something inside her is grateful for Ronee's affection for her music. Maybe it's fate's subtle reins but a decision balance inside her mind wins the day and, internally, she decides to check the idea out. She wanders back to the table with Ronee. Ronee sits down as Lucy asks,

'What can I get you guys?'

Mike Remo smiles, Don smiles at Ronee and Marv looks as if his mind is busy trying to recollect how come he recognises Lucy. They order beer and burgers. Ronee smiles,

'Hey Mike – give LuLu a slot at the all-dayer? She's got some great little songs.'

Mike smiles at Lucy, 'Yes I remember', he pauses thoughtfully, 'Are you up for it?'

Lucy's internal voices raise a frantic debate as she hears her external voice calmly respond, 'Yeh, for sure!'

She shocks herself with the confident tone her voice strikes as she thinks 'WTF am I doing?'

Mike seems pleased and Lucy loves his calmness. She is confident in his ordinances. Mike explains, 'It's over in Sausalito and it would be good to add in a few Stevie Nicks type songs? That would appeal to the audience we're likely to draw over there?'

Lucy nods, liking the idea. Lucy had actually gone over to Sausalito one day and searched for Sound City where Stevie had recorded with Fleetwood Mac. She loved rock and roll history and was drawn to the idea of walking in the footsteps of the greats. Ronee enthuses, 'It'll be a good day out!'

Lucy nods and thanks Mike. She notices Marv looking at her and wonders if he has unloaded The Dog yet. There is a short silence before she spins and returns to the bar. Lucy's mind races as she draws the beers. The SnakeDoubts return to her mind. What if Mike Remo publicises the gig somehow. What if her picture gets onto the mainstream. Inwardly she speaks to herself,

'They didn't know much about me though? It never made national news? I could be anywhere in the world by now?'

Whatever logic she applied to her situation couldn't completely remove the SnakeThreat. She resigned to it and took the beers over. As she put them on the table Marv suddenly remembered her,

'The girl with The Dog!!!! Man I knew I knew you from somewhere!'

Lucy finds herself smiling; there is something likeable about Marv although she can't work out what on the earth it might be. He seems like an absent minded Iggy Pop.

'That's me. Did you get rid of it?'

'Not yet. We thought we'd keep it under wraps for a while increase its antique value!', Marv's face in a wry smile now. Lucy finds herself smiling back. She tries to reinforce the message that it was never hers and had come from an out of town guy. Marv laughs,

'You building a truck theft empire? I run a clean business!'

The whole table looks at Marv in disbelief. Don pats his shoulder, 'Sure you do Marv!'

They raise their glasses, 'Here's to business!'

Marv smiles, 'Don't worry Missy. It's a lost dog!'

Lucy feels strangely re-assured. She reminds herself that she has a lot to thank Marv and Don for. She giggles once again as she thinks of them as her 'Guardian Angels'. Marv looks after her cars, Don looks after her accommodation and Mike is her music manager. She is well set now. What can possibly go wrong?

*

Mike Remo's all day session sits heavy in Lucy's mind until the day arrives and she seems strangely calm. She welcomes the challenge. She thinks to herself,

'Wouldn't it be Sod's Law to find fame when I really don't want it!'

Her Dad has a physics theory to explain 'Sod's Law' saying it is a mathematical inevitability that is a corollary of a theorem of Chaos Theory. An Entropy Wormhole. She thinks of her Dad as she packs Nick Lucas into his case. She and Ronee enjoy the trip across town to Fisherman's Wharf and then by ferry to Sausalito. The fresh sea air seems to easily fill her lungs ready to sing.

Arriving at a busy venue a variety revellers fill the space and there is a nice atmosphere. Mike Remo gives Lucy and Ronee beer tokens and Ronee gets the beers whilst Lucy sits at a stageside table. She scans the crowd for anyone she might recognise. The only one she does recognise is James as he sits on the opposite side of the table. He looks at her and looks away as she smiles. She is embarrassed to remember their last conversation at the gig in Castro. She admonishes herself for her spikiness on that occasion. She tries to think of a way to start a conversation with James as Mike Remo calls him to the stage

'Good evening DirtKickers ...'

Audience cheers

'There will be 3 sets tonight, one from us and then one from the lovely Lucy Smith, and one from both!'

'We are going to start with a song by our friend from over in little old England Mr Jimmy English ... .there he is on the guitar ... .it's called Sick For The Sixties – and we all are – in fact we are currently building a time machine and Jimmy English is gonna pilot us back to England? We're gonna support The Beatles and school them in the art of Skulk Rock.'

He looks over at James: James starts the song on guitar:

Sick For The Sixties

https://badpeoplethemusical.bandcamp.com/track/sick-for-the-sixties

When the future belonged to the left
Well now there is nothing left

I never ever thought I'd ever get this far
In my old jelly mould car
Morris minor mirror memories show us what we left behind
Before we wasted all that time

And the old generation
Are still longing for their dance band days
Steam train railway station
Taking us all away

We're sick for the sixties
Do you think they miss me?
Build a time machine to take me back
And I won't ever miss the CD
I won't miss reality TV

I'm going to build model aircraft fighters
Well why were the winters much whiter?
In this dream mirror where I look
Was life ever that good?

So blame it on the transistor
Or blame it on ambition
Greed is a whore and you can't resist her
Blame it all on Bob Dylan

We're sick for the sixties
Do you think they miss me?
Build a time machine to take me back
And I won't ever miss the CD
I won't miss reality TV

I'm going to go to university

I'll get a grant and I'll do it for free
And I might save the dead Kennedies
Be in a band with Dave Dee, Dozy and Beaky
And then I might fly up to the moon
But most of all I don't want to grow up too soon

The relaxed crowd, the venue and sound are good. Some tourists, some locals all in the mood to listen and drink. The music goes down well. She begins to like The Lowdown Dirtkickers now. She was hasty at the last gig. She reminds herself what a bad judge of character she obviously was/is.

Lucy is suddenly nervous as she sees a photographer moving through the crowd taking pics. As the photographer moves towards the table where she and Ronee sit Lucy retreats outside. There is a large waterfront balcony and Lucy looks out over the bay. She sees Oakland in the distance and the lights of a large container ship slowly moving towards the docks. Gazing up at a bright low slung moon she whispers,

'Are you following me?'

Her vision seems to zoom in on the moon as it hovers. She sees, or imagines she sees, eyeballs staring back at her. She wonders if her father is looking at the same moon through his telescope.

Lucy is still staring at the moon as Ronee's voice interrupts her thoughts,

'Mike says they're ready for you LuLu.'

As she walks back in the noise of the audience chatter is increased and she realises that the audience has swelled during the Dirtkicker set. An army of nervousness masses on her horizon yet, somehow, a calm resolve descends over her mental defences and she remembers what an experienced musician friend once told her,

'When you get to the stage it's your gig, your gig and no-one elses! No room for uncertainty!'

Mike Remo calmly escorts her to the stage and sets the microphone for her. She elects to stand. Mike tells her he will oversee the sound as she tunes her guitar. Now she hears her own voice over the PA system. Lucy plays a short set on her own before the Dirtkickers join her and busk some of her songs. The set goes well and Mike Remo let's her take centre stage when it comes to a final

encore. Lucy introduces the song,
'This song is called 'Stealing Stars".

Stealing Stars

https://badpeoplethemusical.bandcamp.com/track/stealing-stars

The night breeze is a welcome guest
It carries the scent of your breath
The only freedom for a slave tonight is death
And I am Spartacus – nailed to a cross
All that's left of us – is the time that we lost

Do you believe in ghosts like you are never alone?
Do you hear footsteps following you?
On your way home?
And do moments like these – always end too soon?
And life turns lonely and you're howling at the moon

I been in your mind and I know what you been dreaming of
Take whatever I can find – I don't need to be in love
I got stolen stars I left behind – that was my only crime
Memories that I rewind – now I gotta do the time
I see clouds floating by – and rain from the fallen sky
I'm so glad I learned to fly but I never meant to get this high

Years disappear into memories
Stuck in my mind for centuries
Comets return after hundreds of years
Planets spin around like lost and lonely spheres
We're all just a prisoners of gravity

But memories like these can keep you in orbit for a lifetime
Like a sad country ghost over a Nashville Skyline
And those old records spin around inside my mind
Music is the key to travelling back in time

I been in your mind and I know what you been dreaming of
I travel in time and I don't need to be in love
I want to use words to you that no-one ever defined
I got stolen stars in my mind – memories that I rewind

Gradually audience noise subsides and Lucy realises they have the audience now. Nick Lucas feels alive in her hands. As she plays the intro she sees Howard and Elizabeth. Her voice rings now and she senses everything is right somehow. The Dirtkickers get the song straight away. Lucy loves the groove. By the key change break in the song the audience are silent. She looks around at the band as if to thank them. Her eyes meet those of James. She smiles.

The applause is good and eventually attenuates as remnants of sound escape the venue and drift out across the bay. The moon looks down until a single dark cloud stains the sky and drifts across to conceal its bright beauty.

Lucy now sits back at the table. She mentally checks that she has carefully packed Nick Lucas away and she runs a visual check that the case is still where she left it. Organisers are busy chatting to Mike Remo, Thunderman walks outside with Ronee. The Metro-Gnome begins to dismantle his drumkit. The stage is being cleared. A 'jolly' audience member walks over and smiles at her,

'Really enjoyed your set. Thank you!'

She thanks him for listening and is suddenly aware of James sitting down next to her with 2 beers.

'Thought you might like a beer?'

She smiles, 'Most certainly I would. You guys carried a good show tonight.'

'We rock. It's Dirtkicker Skulk Rock', he smiles and juts out his chest. She laughs,

'Are you top of the Skulk Rock charts?'

'We most definitely are tonight.'

'Who is number 2 in the Skulk Rock charts?'

'There isn't a number 2, such is our dominance the genre!', he smiles and adds 'But you went really well. Lit by the moon I noticed', he points up to the rooflights as the moon is now becoming visible through trailing wisps of black cloud. It seems to sit over the venue. Lucy feels a cold sweat.

She nervously looks down at her hands on her knees. James continues

'You play Moon Rock?', he nervously laughs and she smiles.

'I do, the Moon seems to follow me. It watches everything I do.'

'We never get those moons in Manchester England.'

'You're from Manchester?'

'Yes, didn't the accent give me away?'

'Well', she giggles, 'I worked out you are not from round here.'

'Is it that obvious? Even after more than two years?'

'I met another guy from Manchester up in Oregon. He is called Bob! Do you know him?'

James smiles, 'errrrrrm is that Bob Throb the bass player?'

Lucy smiles back, 'Errrrrrm no. This guy plays sax.'

'Oh that would be my Uncle Bob.'

They both laugh. Lucy takes a long sip of her beer, then, 'You must know Morrissey though?'

'Well of course! We were big mates growing up.'

James beams as he recites, "We may be hidden by rags

But we have something they'll never have".

Now Lucy's smile opens up, 'I do love your accent.'

James is emboldened now and goes into his John Cooper Clarke riff,

"Outside the takeaway Saturday night

A blad adolescent asked me out for a fight

He was no bigger than a twopenny fart

He was a deft exponent of the martial arts"

Maybe this was a bridge too far? Lucy stares at him in bewilderment, as if he is speaking a strange dialect from a strange planet at the outermost edge of a distant galaxy. She lets it hang until she sees James struggling to think of something to say to keep afloat in this conversation.

They both break into laughter at the same moment. As they look up Ronee and Thunderman are stood there looking down at them. Mike Remo and The Gnome join the table as they all cool down after the gig. Lucy has known band life in the past but never like this. There is fun and relaxation in the air. They talk of Skulk Rock and how it will be the next wave. Mike Remo is somehow a source of energy; a sun they all orbit around. Lucy begins to feel happy in the sphere of The Dirtkickers. She talks music with James. She looks across at Ronee and sees her holding TMan's hand. The organisers send jugs of beer over. The snake shadows in Lucy's mind retreat to the outer reaches of her thought galaxy.

They all travel back in the Dirtkicker Van. Lucy and James between drum cases and amps and Ronee and Thunderman between PA cabs. The Gnome and Mike are upfront. The van sways in the crosswind of The Golden Gate. At least Lucy hopes it is that and not The Gnome's erratic driving? A few corners and hills pass and the van stops. The rear doors are opened by The Gnome doing his strange dance. Lucy giggles. The Gnome sings,

'Here we are at the lowdown lair of The Bassman.'

TMan and Ronee stand. He passes his bass case down to The Gnome and helps Ronee down. Ronee turns to Lucy smiling. They all smile.

Before closing the rear doors The Gnome smiles,

'Next stop the lair of The Limey!'

The van sways and climbs on hills before lurching to a standstill. This time Mike Remo opens the rear doors. Lucy finds herself holding James' hand as he helps her down. Mike reaches into the van and passes Lucy her guitar case. He looks at her,

'We can run you over to Haight if you like?'

She smiles, 'It's ok thanks Mike. And …thanks for the gig. Thnx-alot.' She walks over and kisses his cheek as Mike stares at James over her shoulder.

As the van pulls away up the hill Lucy and James climb the stairs to his 'penthouse flat'.

10

Pacific Heights

James' flat is one large room with a kitchen area in one corner and a bed in the other. Lucy puts Nick Lucas, in his guitar case, against a wall. She sits at a table and stares through the skylight window. James walks over to explain how he has always loved the view out over the bay but he is stopped in his tracks by the sight of the moon looking like he has never seen it before. He stares too now,

'Firk me!'

Lucy smiles at him, 'It's a Blood Moon!'

'What's a blood moon?'

'Some kind of eclipse. My Dad told me about it once a few years back. They don't happen often.'

The moon just hangs looking so close. James' mind returns to his school physics. Gravity always captivated him. 'We're all prisoners of gravity.' Looking at this moon he finds it hard to comprehend orbits. It just hangs, there must be another explanation? He asks Lucy if she'd like a cup of tea. She nods absentmindedly. As he waits for the kettle he stares at the moon too. Both in silence now. He adds the boiling water to the loose tea in his trusty teapot and breaks the silence,

'It must be some kind of sign?'

She doesn't respond as he places a cup of tea next to her hand on the table.

She breaks into a Morrissey song, "Mother I can feel the earth falling over my head".

James picks up on her change of mood and tries to resurrect their earlier Morrissey conversation

'Loved his version of Moon River?'

Lucy stares and begins to speak, her tone different now, 'Where I was staying in Montana, the moons were so so bright, the moonlings see everything on the earth.'

James laughs 'Moonlings!'

Lucy laughs too 'They can't be subpoenaed.'

He thinks, 'What beer was she drinking?', before asking, 'What could they tell?'

There's no response. The Blood Moon dominates.

'What did you do in Montana Lucy?'

'I was a farmer!'

'A FARMER?'

'Well a farmer's wife.'

'You're married?'

'I thought I was.'

'What happened?'

'He died.'

'Oh wow, sorry.'

'Don't be.'

James looks puzzled. There's a pause. A long pause. Eventually he asks,

'What happened?'

She takes a sip of tea

'Ask the moonlings!'

'Do you have their number?'

He inwardly smiles as he finally gets another half smile from her.

'Nobody does, luckily for me.'

James looks puzzled

'Ah-Haaaa, so they could incriminate you?'

Lucy looks out of the window, a tear runs down her cheek, followed by more tears.

James looks horror struck. He holds her.

'Oh no I'm so sorry.'

'Don't be.'

'I am!'

'Don't be!'

'How could I be so insensitive?', (He thinks to himself 'I sound like Hugh Fucking Grant here?')

'You're a guy.'

'Look I'm sorry.'

'DON'T BE!'

'Why not?'

'I killed the fucker!'

James drops his drink. She stares at the moon unnoticing.

In the time it takes him to towel up the mess and pour himself another cup, she still stares.

'No one else knows that!'

James is speechless. He stares with her. The Blood Moon hangs.

Lucy turns from the moon, her face stained red from the reflected light. She is in floods of tears now. Her mind whirlpools. Blind panic thoughts for having blurted. A voice inside asks her 'Why?' She tries to control herself. Part of her feels easier for having confessed to someone. Why hadn't she fully confessed to Ronee? Ronee has done so much for her. She realises she must tell Ronee. She will. Later.

James hugs her. He looks in shock. Eventually asks,

'Are you on the run?'

'Kinda.'

'Want to tell me about it?'

Lucy gathers herself.

'Wellllll … .Seth was brilliant at first. I met him singing in a bar. I was on a trip west.. He was a talented musician, could play anything. He was the youngest of a musical family. … Trouble was the family.'

'How so?'

'You name it. Anything bad in Montana they were into. Seth convinced me he was trying to get out of the family but over the months after our marriage he was drawn back in. Slowly, nice Seth turned into Seth Snake.'

'Seth Snake?'

'Yes that was their family name! There was Mrs Snake, King Snake, and 2 brothers and a sister.'

'King Snake?'

'That was his Dad. A real skincrawling evil sonoffabitch. I only met him a couple of times, I wouldn't ever go back to their farm after that.'

'But you lived on a farm?'

'Seth had a farm, they all had farms. King Snake bought them all farms. Apparently land is cheap in certain parts of Montana and it is some kind of way of laundering money.'

'Sounds like it could have been good?'

'Well the farm was a struggle but at first it was fun. Seth and I used to get out singing and did some songwriting together. It was fun to try farming too. But more and more he was drawn back into the family band. They were all good and did wild wild gigs. He started coming back drunk and saying the money was in rock and roll covers … and he did make money – a lot.'

James sighs, 'He's right there!'

'Sadly, but there could be a jackpot in songwriting. If you do covers you are a Karaoke singer, do your own stuff and you are in the big game?'

'I agree with you Lucy!'

'Seth didn't and it just got gradually worse. We fought and I got hurt one time.'

She shows James a long cut scar on her upper arm.

'He did that?'

'Yes, the whole rotten family carry knives. And worse!'

'Why did you stay?'

'I was planning to leave but I think he realised. Anyway he hurt me bad that time and then, the final time, he came back from a gig and he smashed my guitar on purpose.'

'That does demand the death penalty!'

'Well that's what he got!'

'ShitFuck Lucy!'

'Will teach him to leave guns round the house!'

'But how come you are in SF now?'

'I came in his truck!'

'But what about the police?'

'I very much doubt that The Snakes would call the police, but they will be looking for me', she inadvertently looks around nervously.

'It's a long way from Montana?'

'Possibly not long enough.'

'How did you get here?'

'I drove in his truck.'

'Can't they trace it?'

'Well no-one outside the family knew he had it, it was an 'acquisition' but he'd spent years working on it. On and off. It got me here ok.'

'But where is it now?'

'I sold it to a garage guy over in Haight. The guy promised me he had a confidential client and would never advertise it anywhere.'

James looks thoughtful.

'Did you trust him?'

'He seemed trustworthy?' Lucy looks nervous again.

'You should be ok then?'

Lucy gets tearful, 'It's always following me, like a night shadow, like a black cloud, like a death eagle.'

James hugs her.

Outside the Blood Moon still hangs now with two bright stars for company.

*

Lucy's eyes open wide in shock as a painfully loud seagull makes a threatening sound. She sees sunlight streaming in through the loft window. She sees the Nick Lucas case leaning against a wall as she senses James in bed behind her. It's a small bed and James is awake gazing at her hair over an exposed shoulder.

'Coffee or tea?', he asks, unsure of what to say.

'Tea? What the fuck is this tea shit? I really have spent the night with a goddam fuckin limey!!'

James is marooned in embarrassment for a moment before she smiles, 'Coffee please.'

They both laugh. James makes coffee and the bright spring morning and coffee aroma makes Lucy feel almost happy. She thinks of Ronee, she thinks of Howard and Elizabeth, she thinks of English Bob. The seagull caws and its shadow moves across a sunlit wall as it moves in front of the loft light window. James brings over a coffee and sits at the table smiling over at her.

'Hey Lucy is your guitar a Nick Lucas?'

She smiles, 'Yes – it is.'

'13 frets to the body!', he smiles, half expecting his guitar obsession to be a character flaw in her eyes.

'I knooowwwww!', she extends the syllables to make him feel small. He gains in confidence,

'Bob Dylan had one?'

'I know. I stole it one night after he invited me over to Woodstock.'

James feigns amazement, 'Wow – really?'

'Really!'

He pauses smiling at her, 'That means you're in deep trouble because I want to be a close personal friend of Bob's and this could be my opportunity?'

'You want his number? You wouldn't even get past the dial phase of the conversation!', she points gun fingers at him. As she does she thinks of Howard's parting gift and wonders if James realises his danger. She worries herself by worrying how serious she might me?

'Can I have a go?'

She smiles and nods. James carefully unpacks Nick Lucas. His eyes take in details of the guitar as they scan the body and neck. He tentatively voices a chord and is not disappointed by the complex harmonies that reward him. Lucy sips her coffee.

'Sing me a song about England?'

'Have you ever been to England?'

'No but I might go soon?'

'How so?'

'On the run! Will you marry me so I can get citizenship?'

'Sure!'

She giggles and James adds, 'But not sure you could handle Manchester after SF?'

'You can teach me the language?'

James thinks and slowly recites some more John Cooper Clarke,

"The bloody pubs are bloody dull

The bloody clubs are bloody full

Of bloody girls and bloody guys

With bloody murder in their eyes

A bloody bloke is bloody stabbed

Waiting for a bloody cab

You bloody stay at bloody home

The bloody neighbours bloody moan

Keep the bloody racket down

Stuck in fuckin chicken town"

His 'Maximum Manchester' accent defeats her and she stares at him, 'Maybe you are right! I'll rethink that little plan!'

She smiles as James begins a song.

Cowboy Drunk

https://badpeoplethemusical.bandcamp.com/track/cowboy-drunk

I'm wishing I was back in Manchester
Having a drink with my ancestor
There was not that much to do
But we could always have a few

Now here I am so far out of my comfort zone
I never did want to wind up quite this all alone
Well maybe I should contact home
But I ain't got no mobile telephone

I'm a cowboy drunk
I'm a lone wolf
I lean to the left, I piss to the right
Well hey little baby I can drink all night
But people call me a C...
Crazy guy
They don't ever say why
My heart's so heavy – my head's so light

And here I am in a bar listening to music
And all the people all dancing to it
Well not me me 'cos I'm just on the piss
And I don't even know what day it is

I'm a cowboy drunk
Yeah I'm a lone wolf
I lean to the left and piss to the right
Well hey little baby I drink all night
And people call me a C...
Crazy guy
I don't ever know why
My heart is heavy – my head is light

I'm a cowboy drunk
Yeah I'm a pisshead punk
I gravitate to the left – urinate to the right
I'm a cider samurai

And everybody says he's a C...
Crazy guy
They don't ever say why
My heart is heavy – my head is light
My head is light

She smiles at him as he puts Nick Lucas carefully back in his case.
James fastens the case and looks at her before speaking,

'Hey Lucy, I enjoyed last night.'

She pauses, 'You're just saying that in case I kill you?'

'I think I'm safe, as long as your egg is not spoiled?'

They laugh.

From the window ledge they are startled by the sound from the
window ledge as the seagull takes flight and glides out towards The
Bay. James walks over to the window and watches it glide into the
distance. His gaze meanders from The Island across to Oakland. He
finds himself wondering about Manchester now. He feels a spasm
of guilt as he thinks of his mother and how long it's been since he
wrote or rang.

Lucy says, 'Shit flat but great view!', as she joins him at the
window

James replies, 'There's Sausalito, where we were last night. Fleetwood Mac recorded Rumours over there.'

She gazes out. James ventures 'We could do that Lucy? You be
Stevie!'

She laughs, 'And you'll be Lindsey?'

'I'd love to try.'

'I kinda already had a scary experience writing songs with a
psycho.'

'I'm not a psycho!'

'Neither was Seth, until I got to know him.'

James looks downcast. Lucy looks at him with penetrating eyes
now,

'Anyway, Thunderman told me you had a girlfriend?'

'Thunderman is full of shit!'

'All men are.'

'I doubt that.'

'You doubt it? What? That all men are full of shit or that you have a gf.'

'Both.'

'Oh yeh?', Lucy's tone changes

He smiles, 'Well I doubt all men are full of shit. I think I knew a guy back in Manchester who wasn't. And ... I doubt I have a girlfriend, although, I hoped I did.'

He continues, 'They tease me about Felicia. She appears and disappears.'

Lucy begins to gather her things.

'I like Felicia but I can't give her what she needs. She needs the money.'

Lucy laughs, 'Thunderman said she was a "superbabe from babe planet?" or words to that effect.'

'Thunderman says a lot. He's never short of bullshit! "She's a free spirit".'

Lucy smiles suspiciously. James tries to change the subject, 'How did you meet Ronee anyway?'

'Don Estrada took me over to get a room in her house.'

'Don Estrada? He's a real character!'

'He seems to look after Ronee?'

'OK, well the guys in the band are a bit scared of him!'

'How so? He seems quite caring under his "Angel" guise.'

'What makes you say that?'

'He told me he had to give Thunderman a "talking to" for messing Ronee about!'

James laughs, 'I remember that. TMan was running scared for a long while. Never seen him so pale and quiet!'

'He's taking that risk again then?'

'Seems so. It's a big risk too if what he told me is true?'

'What's that?'

'He told me Don used to be a hitman back in the day!'

Lucy mocks, 'Sure!'

'So you are saying TMan is a bullshitter? Maybe you are the bullshitter LuLu?!'

Lucy is stung by the remark and realises she has gone too far, 'Sorry sorry sorry! Didn't mean to question a skulk rock originator!'

James smiles, 'I should think not!'

They both smile.

James continues in a jovial tone, 'TMan reckons Don used to advertise for business in the hippie press. He worked under the name of "Paul Bearer!!!"'

'Fuck off! Now you are bullshitting me!'

'Ask Mike Remo. He will know.'

Lucy pauses, 'I think probably best not to follow that line of enquiry too far!'

James nods in agreement.

As he muses, Lucy's mood changes rapidly. She finishes gathering her things and prepares to leave. As she reaches the door, Nick Lucas in hand she stops. Stops and thinks and turns and speaks, slowly and the words fall to the floor with slow running gravity,

'Hey Jimmy English. Me, you and moonlings never speak of certain things.'

'No Lucy.'

'Not even under the worst torture imaginable involving hot spiky metal objects and bodily orifices?'

'Not even then.'

'Good, 'cos you know what happens?', she smiles

'I wouldn't want that because I want to see you again?'

She opens the door and steps out, before walking back smiling, 'I'd like that!'

She blows him a kiss and is gone.

An Alcatraz ferry bounces across the bay under vague white clouds heading east as James gazes silently from the window. He wonders about all Lucy told him. It crosses his mind that she is some kind of fantasist and his mind begins to whirl. He tries to imagine her as a 'farmer'? He thinks of her songs and her edgy but beautiful delivery. He makes coffee and watches the day dawn; life wasn't so bad. He resolves to contact his mother today as he searches for some biscuits. He thinks about his life in San Francisco. It's been 7 years now and he feels settled. He had (kind of) achieved a life's ambition to be a musician/songwriter yet where has it got him? His only family is the band. He is happy in the flat but realises that he has little security. If Jimmy Ho, his landlord, finally gets to buy the adjoining property to develop he will need somewhere else to live. Staying in the city could be a problem with rising costs. His thoughts turn to his home in Manchester England. He remembers the leafy woods and green fields of his childhood. He remembers how they were gradually taken over by housing estates. As a child it was good because they played for hours in the part-complete buildings. Collecting balls of putty and developing a cheaper form of paintballing with his friends. Shootouts in part built houses. How they could spend hours trying to start dumper trucks left idle in the evenings. During the daytimes James remembers watching the hod carriers skip along bendy planks ferrying bricks to bricklayers on the scaffolding. Wiry men with a constant cigarette hanging from their lower lips. How he thought it would be one of the best jobs for him to get because he loved mindless tasks that were repetitive and didn't require detailed problem solving. He had always been obsessive about things and was always content to do what others might find repetitive. He thinks about his father and regrets not speaking to him for so long now. He remembers how his father loved the game of tennis and tried to get James interested in it. How he had enjoyed the game before music took over his life. He giggles to himself as he thinks that this trait may have better suited him to tennis than to music. However, a chance listen to an old Bob Dylan single on his friend's old record player had seized his mind. Bob's voice had seemed so beautiful to him and he could never ever understand why people said he was not a good singer. There were whole lifetimes in Bob's voice. A cast of thousands and even more characters in his songs. 'Like A Rolling Stone' had sent James back to folk songs and the guitar and then forward into rock and roll. Even though everyone in his youth had dismissed his musical abilities as a 'craze' he had always loved it. He loved making up songs too but he had massive uncertainties about music. He could improvise and make up original songs but he considered himself useless as a professional musician playing what he had to in a covers band. He also considered himself pretty useless as a guitar player but his punk background had given him a suit of armour and he loved to think 'covers are for karaoke singers when you do your own material you are in the big game!' Here he was a big game hunter looking for that elusive prize. One hit song could make him a living and he would keep on knocking them out until he got there. He had been so so lucky to fall in with The Dirtkickers; a chance crossing of paths on SF's open mic circuit. Mike Remo had become a sort of father figure.

James skips as he wanders around his flat. He thinks of Lucy and then, once again, thinks of all she has told him. Her 'story' whirls in his head. Could it all be true? Could part of it be true? Could any of it be true? The bitch was winding him up? He picks up a guitar and plays; trying to rest his thoughts for a while. He can't concentrate. He gazes at the view. A strange plume of smoke in the north winds its way into the sky. It looks strangely like a snake coiled and raising its head peering into the distance. 'Oh shit it's The Snakes!', he giggles to himself. It's a false giggle though and his mind soon turn serious. Then he pauses in thought. He looks at the weather and decides to take a walk down to an internet café he knows in Chinatown. There is a skip in his step as he meanders across town. He loves San Francisco. In the café with his coffee now, he goes to a PC computer and types in 'Snake Brothers'. The search returns nothing at first. He adds 'Montana' and 'Band' and some YouTube clips appear. He becomes nervous as he presses play.

A shaky camera shows a drummer adjusting a kit before he clicks in a song. The groove is straight but strangely scary with an overdriven Saxophone on top. As the vocal begins James physically recoils from the screen. A 'presence' appears full screen and his countenance is immediate. This weird demon seems to exude malevolence in large dosages as it stalks the area in front of the band and delivers the lyric. It looms even larger during a weird break in the song.

Illinois

https://badpeoplethemusical.bandcamp.com/track/illinois

Synchronicity brought you back to me
But then it took you away
You disappeared when time turned weird
I couldn't think what to say
Some kind of mental void
I was destroyed
I hope you weren't annoyed

But I'm going to find you again one day
And no mistake
No hiding place can ever remain

Outside of my gaze

Going to Illinois I got a bullet to deploy
Law breaking woman broke my heart
She's hanging around on the wrong side of town
She's hiding in the dark
First we find her
And then we remind her
That this is just the start

We're going to find you again one day
And no mistake
No hiding place can ever remain
Outside of my gaze
There's no getting away

You're in the dark matter
I can feel your pull
And this is never over
'til my dream skull is full
Your space is empty
And my time is curved
Your fates have sent me
My orbit swerved

Calling down a curse pick you up in my hearse
The traffic's getting worse
We've been driving round this lowdown town
Now it's nearly sundown
I've got my eyes on
An event horizon
And it's coming my way

I'm going to find you again one day
No mistake
No hiding place can ever remain
Outside of my gaze
We're surfing in on a gravity wave
Get out of the way
'Cos nothing on Earth can get in our way

We're coming today

Going to Illinois I got a bullet to deploy
Law breaking woman broke my heart

James mutters to himself 'So you are 'King Snake?' The whole band seems to exude menace. Each band member, other than King Snake, seems almost blurred as if some evil aura won't allow them to be captured on film. King Snake seems to fade in and out of focus as if tempting the viewer into some altered universe.

James suddenly realises that the lyric relates to them searching for a woman? Could it be Lucy? The lyric implies that their intentions are not likely to be beneficial to that woman either. He looks for a date on the video and sees it's 5 months old and posted after Lucy arrived in San Francisco. James exclaims, in an English accent, 'SonOffABitch' as he wonders if the woman they seek is indeed Lucy? He slumps in his chair, his energy sapped as if he had gazed too long into a Palantir. James would have been lying if he had said he wasn't nervous now. He gets a shivered feeling that forces are gathering. Suddenly, he swims in the cafe in a fevered daze. His energy drained he feels as if he has fought his way back to shore after an evil tide has tried to suck him out into a desolate ocean.

He winds the video back again and this time through the female bass player takes his eye. She doesn't look like the others. Her dark hair hangs loose and curtains her face. She is slim and tall. Striking in a short cut snakeskin jacket over a ragged T-shirt. A tight leather skirt, black tights and heels accentuates her slim athleticism. This is a different sort of snake indeed. King Snake is a muscular cross between a cobra and a rattler for sure. The fruits of a strange entanglement in the depths of hell. The bass player is an athletic snake who can slither at considerable speed where necessary. You wouldn't feel her bite until the paralysis began to take over your body and shut down your life force. Even so, James feels a force of gravitational attraction from her whereas the intense gravity from the rest was of a repulsive nature. Could gravity ever be repulsive? He thought not. His head still swims as his time on the PC computer expired.

The Snakes

The same blood moon reflecting its bloodstained light to Lucy and James hovers above a Montana highway as a black truck rolls through the night. Inside the truck Jake 'King' Snake drives and Edward 'Sly' Snake sits in the passenger seat. Simon 'Si' Snake sits in the rear with their sister 'AJ' Snake who is dozing with her raven dark hair hanging down and obscuring her face. The truck slows and stops in the middle of the empty highway. The silhouette of a deer is visible on the crest of a rise ahead. The drivers window silently glides down and a King Snake's muscular tattooed arm holding some sort of firearm appears. The gun makes a dry clacking sound as if a woodpecker is nearby. AJ wakes with a jolt. Bullets fizz on the road around the deer and it staggers before falling to the ground. The truck draws forward and King, Sly and Si exit the truck and load the deer carcass onto a rack on the bonnet. Si Snake enthuses, 'YeeHaaa Pa you cant miss with those woodpecker guns!' His compliments fall flat as they climb back into the truck.

The truck rolls away again before swinging off the highway into a large farmstead. The occupants all walk silently into a rambling farmhouse. The premises large and tidy with a strange mixture of modern and traditional furniture. A contrasting variety of vintage musical instruments and weaponry are sitting around. King Snake is menacingly silent. As they each slide away towards different parts of the house King snarls, 'Tomorrow I want a progress report.' His tone is calm, his voice embodied with a strange accent and a slight hiss to it. His eyes follow AJ, looking her up and down, as she silently walks away along a corridor. King slowly walks after her but turns into another room where a slim woman sits at the dressing table slowly brushing her hair. He hisses as he slowly closes the door.

*

As a lowdown morning sunlight streams into the large central room Sly, Si and AJ now sit at computer screens that look strangely out of place. King stalks impatiently around eventually picking up a hefty modern handgun. He pauses for thought, idly pointing the gun at AJ Snake, 'How come we don't know nuthin about the bitch?', he pulls the trigger and the empty gun clicks. AJ Snake flinches. Si Snake laughs at her discomfort and answers for her,

'You know Seth used his fake id to get married in Vegas Pa!'

'The bitch must've done the same because that trail went cold too.'

'So we still know nuthin?'

'We ought to ask the po-lice for more help Pa?'

'And risk them taking an interest in us? How dumb are you?'

King Snake continues, 'I pay the goddam sheriff enough every year but somehow I don't think he could ignore a murder? I asked him to try and trace the truck and the bitch but with such a common name he has found Jack-Shit-All. No sign of the truck either.'

Edward 'Sly' Snake speaking from behind a PC computer in the corner ventures, 'We're workin on it Pa.' King doesn't look impressed,

'Sly Fuckin Snake! And I was thinking of putting you in charge of family shit so I could concentrate on acquiring more land from Fort Peck. A wizard on computers? Don't mess with my mind. I thought you could track anyone these days?'

'We need something to go on Pa!'

Mrs Snake enters the room. Although older she is a striking woman. Slim and tall, she looks incongruous amongst the others. Mrs Snake's hair is solid black and collar length and she wears elegant heels. King looks at her

'And what the fuck do you know my sexy Sioux? You spoke to her more than once?'

Mrs Snake stares him back, 'I know she made Seth happy for a while Jake. And my people are Assiniboine!'

'He's not happy now is he? He is fuckin dead. Burnt to a burger in a house worth a rucksack full of cash.'

Mrs Snake looks sadly down, 'We've been over this a million times Jake. She mentioned Illinois and the cold winters. I think her name was Smith.'

Sly Snake shouts over, 'There's 87 thousand Smiths in Illinois Ma. I've tried a million searches and if I add music all I get is some weasly English band called The Smiths?'

Mrs Snake asks, 'What about the police?'

King slowly walks over to Mrs Snake and a silence envelops the room. He grabs her by the throat. The Snake family look on in silence. Mrs Snake turns red in the face before he releases her. She coughs and gasps, staggering on her heels, before regaining her composure.

Sly suddenly exclaims, 'California.'

King mimics, 'Cali-fuckin-fornia … .Cali-fuckin-fornia … fuckin Cali-fuckin-fornia …'

Sly Snake shouts over, 'SAN FRANCISCO.'

King looks over, 'Los Angeles, San Diego, Oakland, Sacramento.'

'No Pa, there's a truck like Seth's truck on ebay. Location says San Francisco.'

King walks over and gazes at the screen, Sly shows him the various pics.

'Re-sprayed but that could be it?'

'Got ya! The bitch is gonna die slowly!!!'

King instructs Sly, 'Get onto our agent and tell him to book us some gigs in SanFrancisco. It's about time those CityBillies learned about real music!'

Si asks, 'Can we film her end Pa?'

King looks over, 'For once a senssssible ssssugestion.'

King walks to a polished mahogany cabinet and opens it. Inside, a variety of ornamental knives are displayed. King picks a favourite knife and hisses 'We are Bad People.'

'Mad, bad and on our way to the bay!', Sly enthuses.

Mrs Snake slowly leaves the room as The Snakes crowd around the PC. In a sparsely furnished room she picks up a vintage Harmony Stratotone electric guitar which looks so out of place over her black panelled cocktail dress. She plugs it into a battered old Fender Tweed Amplifier and waits for the valves to come to operating temperature. Her slender fingers excite the strings and a spiky, resonant, harmonically rich, texture of air waves is generated. She idly picks out some melodic chords before the door opens again and King Snake's shadow invades the room,

'I'll need you in the bedroom in 45 minutes. Wearing all black for Seth.'

Mrs Snake mutes the guitar. A tear runs down her heavily made up face. She slowly resigns and moves to a cupboard, opens the doors, and removes an aluminium case. She opens the case and retrieves a rubber tourniquet placing it carefully around her upper left arm. As she finds a suitable vein the concentrated expression on her face slowly changes. Although the tension in her face relaxes, her face seems to age. She packs away the stainless steel syringe and sinks into a chair and slowly extracts a gold chain from her bosom. At the end of the chain is a semi-opaque stone. She stares into it whispering in a native dialect. She replaces the stone inside her dress and picks up her guitar once again.

Prison Ground

https://badpeoplethemusical.bandcamp.com/track/prison-ground

I spit on the graveyard wall
When I'm walking to town
That's where your spirit crawls
Under the prison ground

Frost sparkles all around
Like diamonds in the dark
Does it get to six feet down?
And does it warm your cold heart?

Stars were deep in darkness
That you painted on the skies
You were the one that drowned us
In the pisswater of your lies

So bury me with another name
In a cloak and with a knife
I'm scared that I might meet you again
In the afterlife

I wore your necklace
I wore it with no pride

And the devil he never left us
He was at your side

You poisoned my body
You said I was yours to lend
You said I was your property
When you lent me to your friends
The shivers of your dark demands
Are still shaking in my hands
I'm know you will understand
I need another man

So bury me with another name
In a cloak and with a knife
I'm scared that I might meet you again
In the afterlife

Again, I'll never be your whore
Again, I'll never be your wife
I don't ever want to see you again
Not even in the afterlife
Not even in the afterlife
Not even in the afterlife

As she plays the song a dream sequence runs in her mind. Cold stone ruins, graveyard walls and tombstones. In the distance she sees a native American sitting on a horse. His headdress and feathered spear easily recognisable in silhouette against the setting sun. Mrs Snake stares at him. As her dream zooms over the high plains and swoops down to the indian's face it is clearly revealed as an eagle's face.

Thought-visions now race through days when sun burns desert rocks and nights when a cold clear moon fires light down and frost sparkles.

She shudders now as her thoughts blur and refocus on a beach with an overturned truck. She sees bodies laid out on the beach and the incoming tide washing over them. Slowly they turn to snakes and slither away into the sea.

Mrs Snake looks at the clock ticking around and steals herself to go to King.

'Ooljee Ooljee', she speaks her own name as if to call herself to a place of safety. She looks into the mirror and adjusts her makeup. She looks at herself now in a full length mirror, checks her dress. She smiles at her slim figure and shapely legs in the black heels. As she turns AJ Snake is watching her from the doorway. Mrs Snake smiles at her daughter. Ooljee embraces her daughter as they pass, AJ whispers in a low hiss

'I hate him Ma!'

'Ajei my daughter. He owns us. We were sold into this and, believe me, it is better than the alternative was', but then Ooljee closes her eyes in despair and whispers to her daughter, 'The spirits are protecting us daughter.'

'They scare me Ma', Ajei is near to tears, 'they killed a dear for no reason.'

'Never let it show Ajei. The white man senses fear and takes advantage.'

'They enjoy killing?'

'They have brought life and death.'

'My skin crawls across my back at their greed.'

'This earth will allow so much but then it will shed them like fleas. The white man has no vision. They don't respect the earth and they don't respect the earth they leave for their children.'

'They are going to travel to San Francisco?'

'Most probably. They have lost one of their own and his evil spirit has grown into his whole being.'

'I sense him looking at me Mother?'

'That would be his death Ajei. He knows that.'

'We need to escape.'

Ooljee tries to reassure, 'the moons tell me things will change daughter', she pauses, 'Soon! I feel the great spirit watching.'

Ajei looks impatiently at her mother, 'The Great Spirit had better stop fucking around mother! This bullshit has gone far enough?'

Ooljee smiles as she waves a finger and shakes her head, 'You have spent too much time in the parasite white man's world daughter.'

They both laugh quietly as they hear King shouting and Mrs Snake hugs her daughter one more time before slowly walking away down the passageway towards the bedroom. Ajei wipes away a tear and picks up her mother's guitar.

***

A full golden eagle swoops from a streaked grey sky and lands in a singular tall tree somewhere in the Montana Plains. It stares down to two native Indian figures in full tribal wear. The younger figure is Ooljee and the elder figure wears a full headdress. They speak in strange dialect as if to the eagle. Presently two smaller birds appear in the distance and approach the tree with a wavering flight against the breeze. The two ravens land on a branch nearby the eagle. As the ravens land, the elder figure below moistens a finger in his mouth and then dips it into a leather pouch. He then puts the finger, now coated in a redbrown powder into his mouth again. The three birds are still as his incantations increase. Ooljee bows her head with arms outstretched. The elder rises to a long sustained wail now with a vibrato that soars on the wind.

The ravens launch into the breeze and land one on each of Ooljee's outstretched arms. She remains still as the eagle now launches and drops to the ground some fifteen feet in front of her. The elder now speaks again in the dialect but his voice elevated in pitch. The eagle walks from side to side as if considering a proposition. Ooljee now sings too, her voice heavy with emotion. The two ravens stare at the sides of her face. As the elder and Ooljee fall silent, the eagle lets out a call and the ravens take to the air. The eagle stares at the elder and Ooljee in turn and then takes to the air itself. They watch as it circles higher and higher looking for a thermal current. Suddenly, it succeeds and rises quickly becoming a dot in the grey sky. They watch as it swings westwards and disappears towards the horizon.

'The new humans are a problem daughter.'

'We know that father. The worry now is Ajei.'

'We have sent the followers to watch her and to find the white girl.'

'I think only of Ajei. I've seen The Snake looking at her.'

'The spirits tell me that The Snakes will pass.'

'Will it be soon enough father?'

'The damage the new humans do will one day end. The earth

will rid the plains and mountains of them. Their wicked machines that burn the air and choke their own children will kill them all. Their cities will crumble. Some of them have love in them but the force of greed rises too high within them. They have it within them to foresee their own end but still they do nothing. Their thinking is lost. They worship fake gods. Evil machines have grown them to too many. We can only watch Ooljee my daughter.'

'The Snake is a wicked being father. I am weary of his presence.'

'Our people have made mistakes too daughter and your need to be with him is the greatest sadness of my heart.'

'I survive father but I cannot survive if Ajei comes to harm.'

He reaches out and places his hands gently on his daughter's shoulders.

'You are the finest daughter a man could ever imagine. Let us hope my visions are not mistaken!'

***

The eagle rises until the white man scar roads become invisible to its vision. its wings now extended and seldom moving it glides westwards and southwards. It looks for dark green patches of tall forest or grey shadows of crags. In the morning it flies at first light and takes a plains rabbit. Sustained, it again climbs and heads south and west. Now it sees more scars below. It can't gain the height to lose them from its sight. It hates the signs of the plague of new humans. The thought of reaching the city has no appeal but agreement has been made. It has agreed to watch over Ajei.

In days it reaches the foothills of the rockies and sees the scars marking human ways through. It stays high on a crag overlooking a main scar passing through the mountains. On day two it sees its quarry. It launches and swoops over the vehicle. It passes over the vehicle unseen a few times; easily using the thermal currents in the mountains to match the vehicles reduced speed on the winding and inclined scar. It sees Ajei sat in the rear. It decides to mark the truck so it can eventually be located in the city.

It picks a spot where the scar runs between crags and swings around. Finally swoops down in front of the vehicle. As it does it sees one of the parasites emerging from the side of the truck. All the better. It unloads directly onto the vehicle and the parasite before sweeping up and into a stall turn over the road. It sees the vehicle travelling on now marked and traceable.

The eagle now uses valuable energy to gain height and is soon riding thermals above the mountains. It heads south and west. It remembers the vast ocean that is out there and the bay city it has flown over once before. The city will be difficult but there are high mountains made by the parasites and it should be possible to survive on top. The ravens will be of assistance too.

12

The Smiths

A compere introduces Lucy to the stage. It's a reasonably well attended gig and she gets a good reception from the assembled audience in the bar. As she takes the stage she sees a clear full moon outside the window.

'Good evening. It seems that every time I play here there is a big fat moon outside. It follows me (giggle)', she tunes her guitar.

***

The same moon also is looks over a mountain highway as The Snake Truck, travelling west, crosses the border from Oregon into California.

'Isn't San Francisco full of computer geeks like Sly Pa?', Si Snake smiles.

'The whole of California is boy!'

'We got many gigs booked?'

'A few, will give us chance to earn some money while we find the bitch?'

'Good thinkin Pa.'

'Someone has to think for you fuckers!'

Sly and Si sing in sweet harmony now, 'Bitch has got it comin, she's goin down. This ain't no love-in, Snakes are com-in to town.'

Above them an eagle wheels across the darkening night sky. its silhouette blurs across the moon. The same moon that Lucy describes to her audience at that very moment. The eagle invokes a strange call as it begins a dive. AJ Snake hears the sound, she's heard it a few times during rare periods in the truck when they don't chatter like demons to each other. As Sly drums on the dash and King and Si sing they are suddenly silenced by a diving eagle swooping low over the road in front, heading directly for the windscreen until ascending at the last moment. The event silences the three men. Si asks,

'Shall I get the woodpecker gun Pa?'

'Sure thing boy!'

Si gets the machine gun and takes a drink from the bottle they have on the go before hanging out of the window with the gun and scanning the evening sky for the eagle. As he turns a shadow flits across him and he draws his head and shoulders back into the truck covered in excrement. The other two Snakes laugh until the smell turns their laughter to swearing. AJ Snake is the only one that hears a bird call in the distance. The truck swerves, momentarily out of control until as it passes signs requesting 'Please Drive Carefully in the Sunshine State'.

***

Well meant applause from a previous song dies away as Lucy announces,

'Here's a cheerful song. This is about lookin death right in the eye and seeing who has the stronger will. We all got it comin' but we all got to fight. We are bad people!'

Around Here

https://badpeoplethemusical.bandcamp.com/track/around-here

There's a sadness around you today
You got the Black Dog on your trail
We gotta keep him at bay
Around here

Cos we need good memories to keep
I get bad dreams if I'm asleep
And it's hard to stay awake
Around here

High ideals hide dirty work
Ugliness in beauty lurks
There's a heart of darkness
Around here

Darkness at the heart of the empire
Politicians just walking the wire

Church has a crooked spire
Around here

He's got a ruthless criminal mind
Hidden behind those eyes that shine
He's a fierce killer with a heart of ice

I was talking to Doctor Death
We were discussing my last breath
He said 'you got a few years yet'
Around here

But we still own your bones
You are gonna die but – all alone
You're too well known
Around here

You got a grim fate in China
When a doomed ocean liner
Out of control and heading your way
You're on a beach in Ty-Phai

This high moon drives me crazy
These timetables delay me
Nobody ever even pays me
Around here

We're on the run – we're always high
We're night shadow on the sky
We've got a darkness in our eyes

Lucy is gaining confidence and looks out into the audience. She looks down to the mosh as she sees a figure push to the front and recognises James. She smiles.

As she enters the quiet phase of the song and confronts 'Dr Death' she straygazes through the window and sees a dark cloud cover the full moon. A concentrated frown dominates her face.

After the gig Lucy is packing up and chatting to some inebriated guys from the audience. They are complimentary. She deals well with their attentions and produces some copies of her CD, even managing to sell a few copies. James catches her eye as he takes a couple of beers to a corner booth.

When her 'fans' move away Lucy brings over Nick Lucas, neatly packed in his case and sits with James.

'Headliner with CD sales now?'

She laughs, 'People can't get enough of me! Only got to sell another seventy five CDs and I'll be in profit.'

'Or wait until a top producer or manager is in the audience? Just a matter of time LuLu!'

She smiles at him.

'Surprised you are here without a bodyguard? I'm a dangerous woman you know!'

'If anything untoward happens to me, like bullet wounds or blunt instruments, there's a letter with all details at my lawyer's!'

Lucy looks at him suspiciously. She holds the look even until he thinks she is serious. Then she lets her expression change to a smile, 'I sometimes use a knife too; no need for bumps or bangs?', she mimics an Italian accent.

He moves to a posh English, 'Oh I say. Let's be civilised here?'

She holds his hand. There is a lull in the conversation. He suddenly remembers, 'Hey I YouTubed The Snake Brothers.'

Her grip tightens. So much so that James snatches his hand away.

'What the FUCK?', she shouts.

Some drinkers in the bar look around. James raises is hands in surrender until the moment passes.

'Calm down Lucy, I only looked.'

'What if they detect a hit from SF? They are unknown outside Montana.'

'They've got 15,000 hits already, that can't all be Montana Mountain Men?'

'They're connected. I'm pretty sure Jake Snake has some kind of drugs business. Don't even think about them! E-R-A-S-E them from your pathetically small English mind!'

James thinks again before speaking, he realises how shocked and nervous she has suddenly become,

'Hey LuLu, I was thinking about this and they are more likely to find you by tracing the truck you sold?'

She looks worried, 'I know, but the guy who bought it told me he would only sell it privately and he had a buyer'.

'Who was that? Can you trust him?'

'Marv of Marv's Motors.'

James laughs, 'Of course! Dumb me! I should've realised when you told me you knew Don Estrada. Marv's Motors; Keeps America Rollin? Over in Dogpatch?'

'Marv's Motors; Keeps America Rollin? Over in Dogpatch?'

'Yes?', she looks quizzical.

'He don't know what day it is most days Lucy!'

'You know him?'

'Everyone knows Marv, we bought the band van off him. He's fixed it a few times since.'

'Now you got me worried.'

James smiles, 'It's cool. Marv is sound as a pound.'

She mimics, 'Sound as a pound. What kind of limey shit is that?'

James ignores her jibe and sits and thinks, 'Why don't I swing by and see if he sold it or what?'

She thinks, and nods 'I'd appreciate that.'

James smiles, 'Glad to be of assistance.'

'It'll make you an accessory after the fact?'

Meaningfully, 'Hey, I'll risk it', Pause, 'Does it mean we're in a relationship?'

'Yes, one built on violence and murder! You dumb limey.'

'We could add love and friendship?'

'That just means you want to fuck me again? I know how the male mind operates.'

James is without words. He looks at her trying to decide if she is serious or winding him up. He sees the 'I've just finished a good gig' look in her eyes and smiles.

Lucy looks at him sarcastically, 'And – what about your super-model girlfriend?'

James looks thoughtful, 'Felicia … I explained that?'

'Not really?'

'Felicia and me are just not compatible. I can't provide what she needs.'

'You weren't that disappointing!'

He manages a laugh as she stares at him.

'Well, all that needs to be accompanied by money, comfort,

clothes, homes, cars, jewels.'

'Materialistic bitch whore!'

'Hey, I am fond of her', James looks away clearly annoyed.

Lucy realises he is phased and she too looks into the distance until she, eventually, breaks the silence (in fake British accent), 'Only joking old boy!'

'I'm afraid Felicia has a boyfriend, a rich one.'

Lucy looks thoughtful, then, 'Why don't you kill him!?'

She smiles but James looks down suddenly (pause), 'I've killed enough people Lucy.'

'Errrrm, no James. I'm the killer, if you remember.'

'Well I got form too.'

'How so?'

James casts his mind back and chooses words carefully.

'Just before I left Manchester I had a big argument with my father.'

'It happens.'

'But this time he tried to take my guitar off me.'

'Always a questionable procedure in a dispute', Lucy agrees.

'I swore at him and he lost his temper and put my guitar in the trash.'

Lucy goes quiet. James continues, 'I just left home. Moved to London for a few months to earn enough to move out here. Before I left I did hear he was in hospital.'

Lucy asks, nervously, 'Was he ok?'

James carries on, lost in memory, 'I never got back home.'

'But, who DID you kill?'

'Him. He died 6 months later.'

Lucy looks thoughtful, then asks, 'What did he die of?'

'He had a breathing problem. My Mum told me it was to do with his work in a factory. That's why he was so concerned about me getting a good job. He didn't want me to work in a factory like him but he also didn't seem to think Skulk Rock was a good career path.'

'Well. You didn't kill him though?'

'Not strictly', James looks tearful.

'You just want to be a bad person like me? You got no chance Jimmy English. I'm a badass whore from the Missouri Breaks. I leave rotting carcasses across this continent. You're just a dumb limey with a conscience.'

James ignores her. Continuing in his thoughts, 'The sad thing is that my Dad really loved his music. He was always playing music from the old musicals.'

The information gains Lucy's full attention and she looks sympathetically now.

She sings,

'There's a bright golden haze on the meadow – There's a bright golden haze on the meadow …The corn is as high as an elephants eye … '

James has started to cry and tries to sing, through the tears, 'And it looks like it's climbing clear up to the sky … '

She holds his hand across the table. As she waits for his attention to return she remembers English Bob.

James regains his composure and goes on, 'He loved Rodgers and Hammerstein. Especially Carousel.'

Lucy sings, 'When I marry Mr Snow …'

He looks at her. Smiling now, 'You know all these musicals too?'

'My Dad liked them too!'

'Dads eh? We have a common bond then Lucy?', he tries to laugh.

'Yes, indeed! We should start a band. We could be called The Smiths!'

James laughs, 'Our favourite band. It would be most fitting.'

Lucy smiles and adds (casually), 'Maybe The Two Smiths?'

They both stare ahead, James goes on, 'I decree that life is simply taking and not giving – England is mine and it owes me a living'.

They sit and stare. Eventually Lucy sings, 'In the room downstairs – We sat and stared'.

James looks at her and laughs, 'Anyone who thinks it is depressing music is a shithead.'

Lucy smiles, 'It's a well known fact!'

'Well it's well known amongst Skulk Rockers.'

'Oh I'm a skulk rocker now am I?'

'I'm afraid so. You passed into the kingdom of Skulk Rock at the gig the other week.'

'Who decides that?'

'I do!'

'There isn't even a Skulk Rock committee?'

'Well, there are various sub-committees but I have been invested with the power to induct any willing females applicants and when appropriate.'

'I'm sure there have been many female applicants too?'

Her eyes narrow and pierce his armour.

'You want another beer?'

'Why not?'

Fourteen Hundred Dollars

James takes a crosstown bus down to the Dogpatch district and walks into Marv's Motors. Marv sees him coming across the yard.

'Hey Jimmy English! You're walkin man! What's with the Dirt-kicker-mobile now that you're walkin? This is America, nobody walks. You gotta put gas in it you know!'

Marv laughs at his own joke.

'Nice one Marv. No it's something else!'

Marv echoes 'No it's something else', in an attempted english accent, 'would I blend in walking down Piccadilly Jimmy English?'

'You sure would Marv. You'd look like you were fresh out of Eton and on your way to a city bank to start work. You'd need a bowler hat though, but it would look good with leather and oil stained denim.'

Marv sticks out his chest and smiles in defiance of the whole world, 'Marv the money man? Make money with Marv?'

'You're surely in the wrong business Marv!'

'So what's your problem in the world of wheels?'

'No real problem Marv but a friend of mine, Lucy, told me you bought a truck off her?'

'A nice little girl from the north and an old Dodge?'

'Yeh, that's the one.'

'Well the first buyer I had lost interest 'cos the gearbox had a warped mind of its own. So I had to change the gearbox out.'

'So you still got it?'

'Well, yes and no. I had to advertise it on the fishing net and I had a guy from out of state who wants it.'

'Marv! Didn't she ask you specifically not to advertise it.'

'I know, but a few months passed and I thought it wouldn't matter no more. I have re-sprayed it and sorted engine and chassis numbers out. I got a cash flow situation Jimmy E.'

'Marv the money man eh?'

'Just a market swing Jimmy. Marv will resurface.'

'Where's the buyer from?'

'He wouldn't say! Didn't like the sound of him to be honest. Sounded like a fuckin' swamp dweller. Crawled out of a drain somewhere. A piece of shit prick end from a sewer pipe if ever I heard one. Not that I like to pre-judge.'

'Did he leave a name?'

'He just said "King"'

James shivers.

'Uh-oh Marv. There's some real bad dudes after little Lucy and that could well be them'.

'Don't worry I won't tell him nuthin.'

'Hold on Marv. I'm talking really bad dudes here!'

'Seen em all Jimmy Boy. Fuck with Marv and you fuck off or fuckin die. Thanks for the warnin though.'

James thinks.

'Hey Marv, let me buy the truck, I'll pay your askin' price and then you tell the bad dudes you sold it to a buyer from out of town somewhere and add in how you had acquired it off a guy from Sacramento. That will make them think it's not the truck they thought it was?'

Marv laughs, 'So you want to be a Dog owner Jimmy?'

James looks at him quizzically but doesn't bother with any follow up questions to delay his intended business. Marv walks him out to the rear yard where there are a group of Angels sat playing cards and having a beer. Marv nods in their direction

'Never too early for a beer at Marv's Motors.'

They find the truck. James notices the missing second 'D' and the 'e' so it really does say 'Dog' on the bonnet.

'So it really is a Dog?'

'Sure thing Jimmy. American engineering. None of your British VW shit.'

'VW is German Marv.'

'Fine by me Jimmy English. $1400 to you. She's a big old heavy gas guzzling Dog though.'

'$1400. FUCK ME Marv that'll clean me out!'

'Rock bottom price James English. That's what I paid for it and you're getting the replacement gearbox into the bargain.'

James thinks. Marv continues, 'I would say that that constitutes a C-A-N-T!'

He beams at James who looks bewildered.

'A Can't Afford Not To. CANT.'

Marv slaps his thighs as he laughs. The infectious laughter reaches James too as he thinks, 'What the fuck has he been on today?'

A chanting builds up behind him and the gathered angels are grunting 'Can't afford not to – Can't afford not to – Can't afford not to … '

The Angels slowly move under the awning to where some musical instruments are strewn about:

$1400

https://badpeoplethemusical.bandcamp.com/track/1400

I got 14 hundred and 14 dollars and 14 cents
It's my life savings but I don't know where it went
So I got weapons – and I got an evil intent
They told me to leave town but I'm still resident

**I just gotta keep running
I got lawmen on my mind**

I like the cemetery – on halloween
I like chemistry – I got a mind full of dreams
I got a Kawasaki – that runs on K-1 Kerosene
I got a bitch – she runs on morphine

**I just gotta keep running
I won't ever do their time**

I look after myself – I don't need to carry a pistol
To use on people who talk and never listen
I take their money – I'm on a mission
And nobody knows my name
'cos I was never christened

**I just gotta keep running
I won't ever do no time**

I just gotta keep runnin
I keep one bullet behind
I keep one bullet behind
I keep one bullet behind

The song begins and James is tapping along to the rhythm. This is a groove tune for sure. Marv himself moves to a vocal mic. The whole 'band' rocks out. Each member has angel charisma. Angel women appear and start dancing. It reminds James of the movie 'Grease' but with more, much more, menace. During the instrumental break a particularly evil looking angel appears and twirls a sawn-off shotgun like a drum majorette. James watches in open jaw amazement. They finish their song and return to cards and drinking as if the interlude never happened.

James smiles as Marv walks back to him, 'OK Marv, you got a deal.'

Marv smiles, 'Marv's Motors – Keeps America Rollin! I just love the "You got a deal" phrase. It's music to my ears Jimmy E.'

'Hey Jimmy E, you should do that song? Me and Michael Remo used to do that one in a band way way back in the day. Want my fuckin royalties though. Marv is a money mad man!'

They walk into the office and Marv fishes the keys from a drawer and throws them across.

'You know I'm good for the money Marv.'

'I know that Jimmy English! And I also know where I can find you if I need to. You got two weeks!'

As James starts the truck he leans out of the window, 'Marv, real bad dudes, you be prepared!'

Marv nods to the Angels, 'Always prepared at Marv's Motors and I can always call for re-inforcements if necessary.'

They shake hands through the truck window. James risks the crosstown drive without papers figuring that it's only a short distance to the Dirtkicker's lock up facility and practise area in Castro. Nevertheless, he takes a back street route to minimise the risk of being pulled over. It's a hot day and the Dog vibrates heavily on the San Francisco inclines. He curses as he misses a gear on the strange gearbox and suddenly feels dizzy and breathless and has to pull over. As he rests, watching a mother and young daughter walk slowly up the hill he puts it down to nervous tension and the heat. His breathlessness slowly fades. He sits for a few moments motionless in thought until his dream-patterns are interrupted by a pair of ravens landing on the bonnet of The Dog. Their feathers luxurious like black rainbows; they seem to stare at him through the windscreen. He shudders. Watching them, transfixed. One launches to the air and he hears it land on the cab roof; its feet audible as it moves about. The call to each other. James remembers a guy in the bar one night telling him how ravens are the most intelligent birds on the planet. How they can work in teams to corner quarry or trick them into death by misadventure on highways. The bonnet raven seems to stare at him holding him in a gaze until it shits a large load onto the Dog bonnet. 'Fuck!', he starts the engine and he sees the two ravens fly up to an overlooking rooftop. He curses them once more as he puts The Dog into first gear and judders away up the incline.

***

As The Dog disappears over the top of the incline the ravens caw to each other. They survey the street before descending to an open trash can. Raven one keeps surveillance until raven two emerges with a roast chicken thrown to the trash half-eaten. The two peck away for long minutes until a new human approaches up the incline. They caw and launch. They spiral slowly upwards charting a course for the area of new human mountains. The tallest building stretches skywards into a misty white cloud. The ravens can't quite achieve that height and settle on a new human mountain that ends just below cloud level. They caw loudly at intervals.

A young child at play on a floor close to the top of the Fremont Apartment Building is fascinated by the misty clouds that form around her building today. The clouds come and go in the breeze. She waits to get glimpses of the facetted Transamerica Building. This time, as a crook in the clouds reveals the tall spire' she sees a large bird perched on the very top. She calls her nanny but the nanny is busy with a vacuum cleaner in another room. She drops her doll as the large bird spreads its wings to become a much larger red-golden bird glimmering in the sunlight penetrating the cloud cover. She watches it launch and glide circles above the cloud before disappearing through the mist. As the nanny enters the room the child turns to face her in surprised excitement, pointing at the clouds below.

The eagle dives through cloud cover and emerges close by the flat top new human mountain where the ravens await. The eagle dwarfs the smaller birds as it makes a running landing behind the building parapet. It walks to a corner area and tosses a carcass and fruit over to the ravens. The ravens caw as if imparting information to the eagle.

***

As James pulls into the parking yard of The Dirtkickers' lockup Mike Remo emerges from the practise room door, 'What the fuck is that Jimmy?'

'Long story Mike.'

James relates some of Lucy's backstory. He leaves out the details of the murder. Mike looks at him suspiciously, 'So just why are these dudes looking for little Lucy?'

'I guess it's that they want their truck back Mike.'

Mike looks unconvinced but leaves it there. He looks at James for a few extended moments.

'You look like a man with problems today Jimmy? You ok?'

'Can't put one foot in front of the other today Mikey. Guess it's my bio-rythms? As they say.'

'Nothing wrong with your limey rhythm!', Mike slaps him on the shoulder.

As they walk into the practise room Mike fixes James a strong coffee. He sits at a desk in the corner and fishes in the top drawer. He turns to Jimmy with a business card.

'I do pay medical insurance for this band Jimmy. Go see this guy and get a check over', Mike hands James a card with a Richmond address on it. James looks puzzled but he knows when not to question what Mike Remo says. Mike adds, "The Doctor" is an old friend and he can be trusted Jimmy. Ring for an appointment and tell him I sent you.'

'Thanks Mike, I will. Are we rehearsing today?'

'We sure are my man. TMan and The Gnome are on their way. Let's finish that Crazy God song of yours?'

James sits back finishes his coffee as they wait. Mike phones around booking some gigs. James tunes up his old Harmony Stratotone Guitar that he acquired in an out of town pawnshop. He still can't believe the tone of this guitar. Made in 63 with hollow body and a 24 inch scale bolt on neck. He often wonders what gives it its sound? Got to be a combination of the Dearmond Goldfoil 'GoldenS' pickup and the hollow body and the short scale. It's a magical formula unbeknownst to Fender and Gibson. Only Skulkers know this. Every time he plugs it in he is rocked by the tones it generates. He plugs it into the old Fender Tweed amp and his low bio-rythms become a distant memory. Mike looks over as James runs the song down and takes out his old Conn alto sax.

'I love the sound of Skulk Rock in the afternoon Jimmy English!'

Presently TMan and The Gnome arrive buzzing as usual. James mics the Tweed amp and adjusts the practice room PA as TMan pulls an almost acoustic tone from his Precision. Mike picks up his saxophone and tells them to 'lay this one back?' Jimmy can sing it:

Crazy God

https://badpeoplethemusical.bandcamp.com/track/crazy-god

Give me fresh enemies – I need a new war zone
I know I'm a dreamer – and I'm the only one
I take my orders – from evil spirits
Life is not for the fainthearted – and I got to live it

Gravity waves – pull us around
I got a close relationship with the ground
I'm working for the agency – Versace and Versace
But don't designer label me – I'm an independent entity
It's a bit arty farty – for me –
Not my kinda party – don't start me

**Crazy crazy …I'm crazy alright
And there's a Crazy God
Sitting in his heaven tonight
I told you – again and again
and again and again and again…**

God loves crazy people –
He makes so many of them

Some situations necessitate – anti-gravity
And I'm learning to levitate – an entire city
I think it will fascinate – the military
So I'd really appreciate – your confidentiality

Gravity waves – at my command
I rule the sea and I rule the land

I see fires – in my new glasses
And I see wires – lowdown informers
I got no secrets – I don't want no-one to know
And I got no places – I don't want no-one to go

I'm crazy crazy …I'm crazy alright
And there's a Crazy God in his heaven tonight
I told you – again and again
and again and again and again…
God loves crazy people –
He makes so many of them

Crazy God is in his heaven -
He's got things to do
He's got crazy ideas for me –
And crazy ideas for you

As the song finishes they look at each other. Mike breaks the silence, 'It's a keeper', he gives James a smile.

The Dirtkickers rehearse a few more songs before Mike tells them, 'That's enough boys. The bar awaits!'

James announces, 'I think I'll miss the bar this time men. Need some sleep.'

Thunderman looks over before his mouth gets into gear, 'Can't take the pace Jimmy English?'

James smiles. TMan continues, 'Been keeping two girlfriends happy again?'

James smiles dismissively. TMan has the energy of a demon for sure and could party all night every night. Mike stops the banter saying, 'You get some rest Jimmy English and make sure you get any pharmaceuticals The Doctor prescribes.'

TMan looks concernedly at Mike as James puts on his overcoat and waves over a weak smile. The door slams in the breeze.

'Not like Little Jimmy English to miss the bar Mike?'

'He don't feel too good. Don't look too good either.'

'He'll be ok for the gig on Friday? He's a tough little limey.'

'He sure will, I sent him to see 'The Doctor'.'

An ominous dischord sound slowly builds as James' plugged in guitar slides down the speaker cabinet where he'd left it leaning with the amp still on. The Dirtkickers look at it in silence as the falling guitar sound decays now. The following silence lasts a short while before Mike walks over and picks up the guitar and switches off the amp. The Gnome breaks the silence,

'Doctor Charlie. Oh yes sir, The Rock and Roll Doctor will put him right. "If you wanna feel real nice – Just ask the rock and roll doctor's advice"'.

Mike switches off the lights as the 3 Dirtkickers leave the lockup. James' amplifier light slowly fades into the silent darkness.

Doctor Charlie

It's a grey but warm San Francisco day as James takes a crosstown bus over to the medical practice to which Mike had sent him. 'The Doctor', or Dr Hubert Charles, is a big personality, big heart and big stature guy whom you would have no wish to disagree with. He has known Mike for a long time. The walls of the waiting room are hung with many interesting photos of jazz combos and it turns out that The Doctor had played drums in various jazz combos way back in the late 50s and early 60s. On one visit The Doctor shows James an old black and white picture of a crowded club with a mosh in front of the stage. A woman singer with a saxophone slung around her slim neck and himself at a drum kit behind her. He laughs as he tells James that it is 'Doctor Charlie's High Rollers' and the singer is Mike Remo's mother.

'Those were different times young man. We played a hard edged drive-jazz–bop-blues. I had a snare sound like a cannon or like a whiplash. I could control a whole room with my snare and kick. Stella Remo could blow too man. She could front any band, handle any situation. No eventuality could phase Stella. She was rock steady. Although my name was on the band she ran it. I loved her too; everyone did. You would not mess with Stella either. She always took a gun to gigs just in case. Saved my butt on more than one occasion', the Doctor took some time out to drift back. His eyelids slowly close.

'Fuckin rock and fuckin roll killed things for us. Then the 60s killed again.'

James had found himself hanging on every word of The Doctor's stories.

'They killed us with Vietnam. I guess they figured a big black guy like me could handle a heavy machine gun. I once shot a tree down thinkin there was an NVA sonbitch behind it. That gun could fuckin rock man!'

'When I came back I was mean. Didn't care nothin'. The music was gone, I couldn't find a band, and I was on too much flake. They used to call me The Black Snowman, The Black Rush or The Dustache. I wasn't gonna play the psychedelic rock shit and I was just low down. I had snakes inside my mind.'

James had even thought of telling The Doctor about The Snakes in his mind. He was sure Doc Charlie could prescribe the necessary? Probably a head shot for each. No messing about.

'It was Stella Remo that got me straight. She asked me to sit in during one of her gigs and I was floating way too high. The gig went a little wild, like the old days, but Stella wasn't pleased. The bitch broke my nose with my own pistol I shot the ceiling to finish a number one time!'

The Doc showed James his bent nose, as if James hadn't already noticed. The Doc smiled as he reminisced.

'She moved into my apartment, with young Mike as well, and got me straight.'

'She stayed while I resumed my training and I really did become a doctor.'

The Doc was lost in memories.

'Until the stars took her', The Doc shut his eyes for a few long moments.

'Mike used to come round for a jam after. I love him like a son but so did his real father. Long story!'

It was obvious that The Doc initially thought James might have a drug related problem this being 'typical of musicians'. James was so impressed by the detail of his examination and felt 'better already', as his Mum always used to say. James had found himself looking forward to his medical appointments as he found the stories of the old jazz days so interesting. On one particular appointment The Doc had seemed 'down'. One of the world's weights seemed to have been cast upon him. James found himself trying to cheer The Doc up. James had been responding well to his medication and his breathing was getting easier. The Doc's reminiscences took him back to Nam again.

'So many of the good guys had to go. We even killed our own. If you think Toot is bad you should know there are worse chemicals. Men who push those chemicals need to be cast down. Fuck those fuckers all the way down. Goddam fuckin dioxin. Evil curse Jimmy.'

The Doc had been asking James about his working life in England before coming to the states. James had told him of the various casual jobs he'd taken in London to earn his passage to the states. Warehouse jobs. Office refurbs in the City of London. His last job had been a clean up in an old power station that was converting to an art gallery. It had been a good earner and it enabled him to save enough for his ticket to America. The Doctor seemed interested in the details and James was happy to reminisce himself this time. The crew he'd worked with had looked after him on the casual work without insurances. He'd felt at home with this band of brothers. He'd even got to live one of his boyhood ambitions to be a hod carrier. He found himself telling the doc of how they used to go for a beer after work in London and how the covering of dust made them look like grey ghosts next to the dark suited bowler hat brigade at the bar.

*

James thought of his old construction gang mates as he took a crosstown bus to the Embarcadero. His excitement was high because he was going to meet Felicia again. She appeared and disappeared but during the latest manifestations they had met more regularly. Her attraction was irresistible. Totally irresistible; the 5th force of nature; an orbit that could not be broken out of. Einstein's theory would have to be modified sooner or later. Some strange new mathematics was going to be necessary. He had felt guilty as he also saw Lucy more and more these days. He felt like a minor planet is some strange orbit around binary stars. The mysterious force of attraction could not be screened. This was strange gravity indeed. He wanders slowly along, stopping to gaze out across the waters as grey clouds begin to give way to spring sunshine. A large container ship crosses the bay and he breaths deeply filling his lungs with the sea air. For the first time in what must be weeks now he even feels hungry.

He walks into Boudin's and upstairs to the restaurant. He scans the clientele for Felicia. The excitement of seeing her never diminishes. He thinks to himself, 'Is she really as perfect as he remembers?' He suddenly sees her stand to beckon him and he realises she truly is. How had he not spotted her straight away? Once seen she is the focus of the whole room. James imagines the envy of the men and women around as he sits down with her. She greets him with a hug and the free electrons in his body race around as they don't know where to go to balance the electro-magnetic-gravity field she generates and that warps all of space time.

'Hey Jimmy English!'

'Hiya Felicia!' (In his best Manchester accent), 'How yer doin?'

'I'm good', she smiles, her teeth not perfect but better than perfect somehow. He longs to run his tongue over them. He breathes deeply savouring the sweetness of her breath. There is no part of Felicia that doesn't pump his heart into an overdrive. He longs to touch her and puts a hand on hers over the table before she breaks the silence, 'It's been a while?'

'Yes. Four weeks, three days and 6 hours. Where have you been?'

'Life's pressures Jimmy!', she giggles, 'How is the Skunk Rock Scene?'

'Errrrrrm, that would be Skulk Rock Miss F!'

She laughs and James has to focus to remain conscious. The room spins. A lifetime comes and goes in his mind. The whole restaurant seems to look at her in that one expanded moment. James slowly swims back to the surface and finds himself gasping for breath,

'Hey, you wouldn't marry me would you?'

She pauses and looks and smiles. The moment extends and extends and a seal barks in the distance. He carries on, 'Just for a week? A day? A night? An hour? And then I'll set you free again by jumping from the Transam building and knowing it has all been worth it.'

She looks at him in a timestop moment before casting her gaze downwards.

'Wellllllllll – funnily enough – I wanted to tell you – I'm getting married next month!'

The words bounce around his skull like a squash ball thudding against heavy concrete. Dioxin descends onto the rainforest of his mind. His mind frantically searches for a new swearword that he can repeat over and over again in the dungeon into which he has just been cast. Was she joking? No, she wouldn't. She must be serious. He tries to wind back time. A leap year passes before he can speak, 'To Rich?'

'Yes, I'm gonna be Mrs Rich Guy!'

He stares at her expressionless as if he has just looked through a telescope brought by Santa Claus only to see a luminous green kryptonite comet heading straight for his doomed planet. He offers, 'Congratulations!'

They look at each other. James breaks the silence, 'This is like a scene from Four Funerals and A Wedding! All the funerals are mine.'

Felicia laughs, 'More like Brief Encounter. Anyway, Hugh Grant doesn't know Skulk Rock from Acid Rock.'

'But he has more money than Rich!'

Felicia looks hurt, 'That's unkind Jimmy English!'

James apologises and Felicia soon smiles again.

'I wouldn't bet on that Jimmy boy. Rich is fuckin rich!!'

'I'm glad for you! I never heard you swear. Swear again, please?'

'Thanks Jimmy', she holds his hand across the table, meaningfully.

She continues, 'What a pity there's more money in real estate than in Skulk Rock!'

'I've noticed that!'

Felicia looks concerned, 'Hey Jimmy E you feel cold and you look pale?'

'I'm ok, just a chill.'

'I got a chill – in Susanville – that first time we met Jimmy!'

James smiles, 'Gave me the shivers until this day Miss F', he feels a tear run down his cheek now.

He thinks and adds, 'Do you need a Skulk Rock Band for the reception?'

She laughs, 'Not sure Rich would go for that and he's paying for it all. His family are a bit nervous of me!'

They look at each other. Felicia ventures, 'We can still be friends once in a while?'

James' replies, 'I would – BUT – I think that I'm in love, but I can't say for sure, that kinda thing is complicated stuff, all I know is I never felt like this before.'

Felicia smiles, 'Who is she?'

'She's a singer friend. She's a real killer Felicia!'

Felicia smiles thinking it's a joke, 'I'm sure she is if she can steal my skulk rocker?'

James feels a hammer drill in his heart. A burning in his brain and a sinking of his soul.

James changes the subject, 'Hey come see us play tomorrow night? It's McMurphy's Irish Bar down in Fillmore somewhere.'

Felicia thinks, 'Well I'm in town with a few girlfriends. So we'll see?'

*

Unbeknownst and above them, grey clouds melt away as the sun in the south illuminates a low slung daytime moon to the north. The two ravens land on the Boudin roof and an eagle crosses the disc of the moon clearly visible in front of a blue sky. Not a soul in San Francisco notices other than a little girl on the pier, her mother proudly looking at her in a new yellow dress. She stares to the sky pointing.

James jumps on an F-Line (rolling south on The Embarcadero) on his way to Dirtkicker HQ to meet the guys before their gig that evening. He thinks of Felicia, he thinks of Lucy and, for some mysterious reason, he doesn't feel down. He feels glad to have been close to Felicia. Strangely, for all her considerable beauty it is her personality he now misses most. Nothing upsets her and she always seems calm yet jovial, light hearted yet attentive, cool yet red-hot, here yet not-here.

'Does the body rule the mind? Or does the mind rule the body?'

He didn't know.

'Felicia Felicia – I'd take a bullet for yer.'

He thinks of Lucy now.

Thunderman is waiting sat on his bass rig repetitively pumping out a dance riff.

'You look downtrodden Jimmy E?'

'Weight of the world TMan.'

'Where you been?'

'Heaven and back. I saw Felicia.'

'I told you she was Too Much For You?', TMan laughs at his own reference to a Dirtkicker song

'Man. She is out of this world.'

'I told you sex with aliens is not generally beneficial.'

'Tell her fiancée!'

'ooooooooooh – fiancée? Is he on your trail? Do I take it she's ditching you?'

'Yes for some arsehole property developer?'

'Who can afford her tennis coach?'

'Probably!'

As they chat The MetroGnome has arrived and listens to the conversation. Thunderman makes a suggestion, 'Hey, in view of Jimmy E's bad news let's try the whores and dwarves song?'

The MetroGnome kicks out a shuffle drum lick and Thunderman drops in before Jimmy English takes up the Guitar and Vocals.

In Bruges

https://badpeoplethemusical.bandcamp.com/track/in-bruges

Well she taught me how to party
With whores and dwarves in Bruges
One kiss was all it took to start me
Now I got something for her that's huge

And I think that I'm in love
But I can't say for sure
That kind of thing is complicated stuff
But all I know is I never felt like this before

My Daddy never told me
Goodbye is the cruelest sound
Women like that are always deadly
Take your heart and nail it to the ground

Well now the sky is upside down
And my life is back to front
And my head is spinning round and round
She's the only thing that I want

But my Daddy never told me
Goodbye is the cruelest sound
Women like that are always deadly

Take your heart and nail it to the ground

Take your brain and wash it
Take your soul – crush it
Take your mouth – kiss on it
Take your heart and piss on it

Well it looks like my nightmare worst fear
That bitch would one day disappear
Now it's kinda like a dream come true
It's the only nightmare I knew

But my Daddy never told me
Goodbye is the cruelest sound
Women like that are always deadly
Take your heart and nail it to the ground

Take your brain – wash it
Take your soul and crush it
Take your mouth – kiss on it
And take your heart and piss on it

As Jimmy E sings Mike Remo arrives and opens his worn leather bound attache case where he keeps his harmonicas. He links into harmonica breaks. The song rocks.

Mike Remo exclaims, 'OK, that's in the set for tomorrow night!'

The Gnome stands behind the drum kit and does his strange dance, 'I lerv it man! Whores and Dwarves my kinda party!'

He carries on dancing as the rest of The Dirtkickers stare at him, 'We should call it 'Whores and Dwarves'?'

'Hey Jimmy E – Are all the parties in England like that? We should do an England tour Mike?'

'Is Limey Land ready for us?'

'Im ready to party!', The Gnome carries on dancing.

James feigns indignance, 'Hey. It's a breakup song!'

'Breaks me up man! Kissing and pissing, whores and dwarves; you're the goddam second Shakespeare!'

TMan giggles, 'This world ain't ready for Skulk Rock. We ARE Bad People.'

Mike Remo confirms, 'We surely are – let's get down the bar!'

*

Deirdre brings over the drinks. She smiles, 'Mike Remo and The Shitkickers? You guys are early tonight?'

They all look intently at Deirdre. Mike proposes the toast, 'Deirdre the waitress. You are cosmic and may you always bring our beers over in this universe and the next.'

She looks at the four of them and smiles before moving off through the bar. Eight eyes follow her.

'Gotta love that Deirdre?'

'Most people have?'

James looks at the other three Dirtkickers and they each look downwards, 'Well I haven't?' James laughs out loud now.

TMan giggles as he changes the focus of the conversation, 'How about a hand of beautiful woman poker?'

James looks confused, 'What the … . is 'beautiful woman poker'?'

TMan explains, 'C'mon Jimmy. This is how it works. You gotta name a famous woman from films or music or whatever who you don't know but who you could 'lerv'?'

He stands and mimics a slow smooch-dance. James stares in amazement.

'Then the next guy has to 'raise' by naming an even more beautiful woman? If nobody 'calls' you then the next guy has to 'raise' again with an even more beautiful woman.'

'So what happens if you get called?'

'Well then it is thrown open to a vote or to an independent adjudicator for a decision of course!'

James thinks and then states, 'This is sexist shit?'

It goes quiet as they all stare at him in silence now until he laughs, 'but I like it!'

TMan sits bolt upright ready to start. He adopts the pose of Rodin's Thinker. Eventually, 'Maureen O'Sullivan?'

James looks confused, 'Who is Maureen O'Sullivan?'

They all look at him in surprise. Mike explains, 'Tarzan's wife Jimmy Boy. Don't you have no culture over there in England?'

They stare at him seriously.

Now the Gnome adopts the pose, 'Errrrrrrrrrm Faye Dunaway!'

TMan asks, 'The young Faye Dunaway from Bonnie and Clyde or the Chinatown Faye Dunaway?'

The Gnome is confident. 'Either?'

No-one calls. They all look at Mike Remo. Mike thinks … .

'Kim Basinger!'

The Gnome shuffles in his seat, 'Ooooooooooh, I dunno Mike, I'm thinking of calling here?'

Mike bluffs him out, 'Call if you like pal? You gotta weigh up sexiness? C'mon The MetroGnome – Call it?'

The Gnome sits back in his chair and they all look at James. James feels the pressure. He feels a bead of sweat on his forehead. A couple of guys leaning on the bar are listening now too. James' mind works overtime until eventually he blurts, 'Gabriella Sabatini.'

The Gnome immediately shouts, 'CALL.'

Tension is high now. Very high. Mike Remo speaks, 'ok gentlemen. The call is Kim Basinger or Gabriella Sabatini?'

He looks at TMan who answers immediately, 'Gabriella', he looks a James smiling.

Mike adds, 'Well I'm for Kim as she was my pick.'

He looks to the two guys at the bar and the both speak as one, 'Gabriella!'

Mike declares, 'Gabriella Sabatini takes it. She's with Jimmy!'

The Gnome sits back in his chair in abject disappointment. He bemoans, 'No, no, no … .'

James is laughing now as he thinks back to his father enthusing about Gabriella Sabatini. His Dad always loved tennis. She was gorgeous though! His Dad once told him that she 'couldn't get enough!' When asked 'How do you know?' his Dad had replied 'I read it in The Daily Mirror!' 'Fair enough', as Shakespeare would say.

'She will be good company', thinks James.

Deirdre brings over the next round and slowly walks away from the table shaking her head in disgust.

TMan starts the next deal with, 'Gina Lollobrigida!'

The Gnome is concentrating hard now.

'Errrrrrrrrrrmmmmmmmmmm … .Sandie Shaw.'

Mike Remo smiles, 'Hmmmmm – something sexy about Sandie for sure', he retreats deep into thought now. Eventually, ' … .Stevie Nicks!!!!'

James' concentrating face is on duty now as he begins to rifle through his mental filing cabinets.

TMan intervenes, 'No point Jimmy!'

'Whaddya mean? It's my turn!'

'No point Jimmy. No-one can beat Stevie Nicks.'

James looks around to the others. TMan asks the question, 'Can anyone beat Stevie Nicks?'

The Gnome shakes his head, Mike shakes his head. The two guys at the bar shake their heads. TMan shakes his head slowly.

'Sorry Jimmy that's one to Michael J Remo. Stevie Nicks is with him!'

James accepts the ruling reluctantly.

It's James' turn to start now. He thinks, ' … .Chrissie Hynde.'

The table goes quiet. The two guys at the bar are quiet. Everyone looks at James. Eventually Mike breaks the silence, 'Ohhhhhh Kayyyyyy … .That's another one to Jimmy English!'

James asks, 'How so?'

TMan slowly explains, 'Well no one can beat Chrissie Hynde!'

James scratches his head laughing now. TMan asks everyone for confirmation, 'Can anyone beat Chrissie Hynde?' Everybody shakes their heads.

James laughs now. Shaking his own head. He thinks and asks, 'What about Stevie Nicks?'

TMan looks at him as silence falls, 'Don't be fucking silly Jimmy English. She's with Mike Remo!'

They rock about laughing. The Gnome pronounces, 'Stevie is not a two-timing bitch Jimmy. How could you suggest such a thing?'

Deirdre appears with a jug of beer now. Shaking her head but laughing too, 'You guys are bad tonight. You are Bad People!'

'Goddam right we are Deirdre. So keep the beers coming on in!'

One guy at the bar asks, 'So what do you guys do?'

The Gnome replies, 'We purvey Skulk Rock to any enlightened listeners in the vicinity.'

TMan adds, 'Fuckin right we do!'

The guy asks, laughing, 'What is Skulk Rock?'

TMan goes on, 'It's original songs with drive, with groove, it's loud, it's soft, it's always got groove, it's new, it's old, it's LoFi from on high and it boldly goes anywhere we take it but it's always got groove!'

The guy laughs and asks, 'So, who are you?'

The Dirtkickers answer as one, 'We're The Lowdown Dirtkickers and we're coming your way.'

The other guy asks, 'So it's not mainstream then?'

The Dirtkickers go quiet now until The Gnome speaks, and with some considerable authority, 'The damage the mainstream does will one day end. The earth will rid the plains and mountains of them. Their wicked machines that burn the air and choke their own children will kill them all. Their cities will crumble. Some of them have love in them but the force of greed rises too high within them. They have it within them to foresee their own end but still they do nothing. Their thinking is lost. They worship fake gods. Evil machines have grown them to too many. We can only watch for now my brethren.'

The two guys at the bar look at each other before declaring, 'That's right The Mascara Snake!'

As the Dirtkickers are teaching the two guys the Skulk Rock salute, Deirdre brings over another jug, 'You fuckers want fucking locking up. And soon!'

Come Running

It's a bright day and Marv walks out into his main workshop. He shakes his head as he sees an angel flat out on the ground, the rising sun sends a shaft of light from a hole in the roof puts the sleeping angel in a spotlight. Marv lightly pushes the toecap of his biker boot into the angel's ribs until he groans.

'Another day another dollar Al!'

Al groans and rolls over. Marv dials in Radio Castro and ambles over and lifts the hood on a V8 Pontiac he is working on. A Low-down Dirtkickers' track is playing and Marv sings along. The bright light from the main doorway is suddenly dimmed by an imposing figure. Marv senses a presence and looks up slowly. King Snake follows his shadow slowly into the workshop. He is followed in turn by Sly and Si.

Marv smiles, 'How can I keep you guys rollin?'

'I phoned about the old Dodge truck?'

Marv frowns, 'Goddam it! I sold it a couple of days ago! You never left me a number? That sonoffabitch was here for months and now two people interested in space of a week. Don't worry man, it was a real Dog and $2500 was a good price! Still you know what they say? A fool and his money are soon parted! You don't look like no fool though mister.'

King is not impressed with Marv's double negative and hisses, 'I fuckin rang you about that vehicle?'

'I remember, you're from a long ways and I didn't think you'd wanna travel for a shitbox vehicle like that? I'd've rung but you didn't leave no number.'

'Who bought it?'

'Some guy from outta town.'

'Who did you buy it off?'

'Some guy from outta town', Marv is beginning to sound annoyed, 'I'm runnin' a business here vehicles come and vehicles go.'

There's a pause. King stares and nods to Sly who walks over to one side. Sly Snake is obviously toting as he wears a long coat on a hot day. Marv looks un-phased, 'So if there's nuthin' else I can help you guys with … .?'

King Snake lets out a slow hiss now and slowly pulls his chosen knife, 'I think your mind is messed right on up with your fuckin' LSD and whatever other shit you stuff up your city boy ass. I'm gonna cut some information out of you', he moves slowly towards Marv.

As King moves slowly forward Marv calmly puts down a spanner and his hand re-appears with holding a Glock 19-9mm, 'What you gonna do shit-kickin country boy, stab my bullets?'

King laughs as Sly and Si Snake produce shotguns. The tension is cut by a voice from a corner door, 'Country boys with knives and guns make me fuckin laugh!'

Don Estrada moves forward from the shadows. He has a Winchester pump in his hands. As he moves forward 3 more Angels appear, each similarly armed and their weapons trained on The Snakes.

'One wrong moves and this place will be like a country butcher's market stall. You wanna end up in Ho Ming Chee's sweet and sour pork stew fat country motherfucker?'

Don moves forward. He sees Si Snake stood looking tense. As he stares at him he raises his voice and shouts, 'Alvin, there's a country Nancy-boy out here that doesn't know he is gay yet. Can you get out here and see to him?'

There's a pause before an overweight and less than good looking angel rushes in and asks, 'Where's that Don?'

King slowly lowers his knife, 'OK Mr Marv, I'm gonna have to believe you for now.'

'Your choice', Marv smiles.

King backs away his hiss becoming a snarl, 'I know you bought that truck offof a bitch called Lucy from Illinois and I know she is still around here and I know she is the walkin dead!'

Marv stares at King Snake without blinking as Don walks forward, his pumpgun trained on King Snake. The Snakes slowly back out of the workshop. More angels appear now and they cover the

Snakes, herding them to their own truck. They keep weaponry trained on the truck until it is out of the gates and moving off up Illinois Street.

Marv let's out a long whistle, 'pheeeewwwwww, thanks boys.'

Al the angel declares, 'You'd be butchered meat without us Marv!'

Marv smiles, 'And you'd be riding pushbikes!'

The tension eases and they all smile.

Don sounds genuinely friendly now as he puts down his weapon and walks over to hug Marv,

'When you need an equation you can depend on Marv?'

'I always come running to you Don Boy.'

The words cue movement in the assembled angels and, as if by instinct, they walk to their musical instruments and begin to play.

Come Running

https://badpeoplethemusical.bandcamp.com/track/come-running

What if positivity can't save you?
When gravity makes you crawl?
What if electricity betrays you?
When you got to make your one last call?

When you feeling that lonely when you feel that all alone
God's looking for you with a nuclear drone
And all your tablets have turned to stone
Come running – come running to me
Come running right back to me

What if your religion is a ball and chain?
What if it never ever brings you back again?
And what if the next world is just the same?
None of your memories remain

What if x-rays can see your thought dreams?
What if they're featured in a medical magazine?
What if the doctor prescribes you pity?
Because you can't handle eternity

So if you're feeling that lonely if you're feeling that all alone
God's looking for you with a nuclear drone
And all your tablets have turned to stone
Come running – come running to me
Come running right back to me

When a Sultan casts you into a dungeon
When you need an equation you can depend on
When you got good reason to join the foreign legion
Come running – come running to me
Come running right back
Come running right back
Come running right back to me

The song rings in Marv's workshop.

Marv and Don dance with each other and their love and relief is obvious. As the song ends and silence takes over they all walk to the tall fridge and grab beer.

'I hate those situations Marv. We're getting too old!'

'Tell me about it Don.'

Marv moves to a couch and sits as the angels disperse keeping an eye on the gate to the yard. Two of them stare down the Snake-Truck as it slowly drives past one more time.

Marv holds his head in his hands, 'Hey Don, is that little Lucy still living with Ronee?'

'Yeh!'

'We better keep a surveillance on that situation?'

Don Estrada's eyes narrow, 'Never have a daughter Marv. They just give you worries!'

He asks, 'Hey Marv, do we have any of those electronic tracker devices still?'

'We sure do.'

'We need to get one on their truck to keep one step ahead?'

Al the angel, is listening, 'Why don't we just kill the shit out of them boss?'

Don and Marv look at each other. 'He's got a point!'

16

Nothing You Can Do

James walks out of Doctor Charlie's medical practice and looks at the blue sky. His mind presents random flashbacks. For some reason he has a desire to see the ocean. He hasn't seen it for some while. He walks two blocks south, crosses Fulton Street and enters The Golden Gate Park. He breathes deep and treasures every breath. He sees birds he has never noticed before. The blue sky seems to be a different blue; deeper, richer and clearer. He wonders if that is down to the drug program Doctor Charlie has put him on recently? He wanders westwards through the park smiling at others. He wonders why he never spent more time over here? Time seems to expand around him and the world suddenly becomes more intense than before. He loses track of time as he wanders past lakes, across the golf course as he begins to smell the ocean air. He sees a windmill in the trees and walks down the hill towards it. Now he hears the ocean too. As he passes the windmill and steps out of the tree line the Pacific Ocean confronts him. Wide and tall rolling waves crash onto the beach encouraged by a westerly wind. He crosses the highway and descends a ramp onto the beach. The warm breeze seems to electrify his skin and yet more memories flash into his mind. He remembers family trips to Blackpool England when he was a kid. He remembers playing football on the beach there with his father. He thinks of his insignificance as he sits on the mostly deserted beach watching the breaking waves. Point break. The phrase 'Nothing You Can Do' jumps into his mind and he begins to sing to himself …

James leaves the beach with a song intact in his mind and his focus now becomes that of getting back to Dirtkickers HQ before he forgets it. His mind solid and focussed now. He sits on a cross-town bus singing the song to himself and hurriedly lets himself into the lockup. He scribbles down the lyric and begins to work on the chords. He wants a defiant groove and more than just a rock/

blues tune. He experiments with key changes and the song appears. He gets the warm contentment of having created something.

As James sits and makes himself a coffee Mike Remo arrives.

'Yo Mr English. You look well.'

'I been on the beach Mike.'

Mike smiles and sings a few lines from Surf's Up. James laughs and tells him about the new song. Mike is keen to run it down. TMan and The Gnome arrive and Mike insists they work on the song. It takes time to tame this one as there are a few sections to it but pretty soon the song is in shape. Thunderman is his usual energetic self,

'Nice song Jimmy E. We were worried about you. You not been your usual self?'

Mike Remo is quiet and gets everyone a beer. They all sit. Thunderman is irrepressible,

'Those two women wearing you out Jimmy?'

James remains quiet as if lost in thought. Mike Remo looks at Thunderman as if to tell him to ease off. James suddenly speaks,

'Something I need to tell you guys.'

'What's that Jimmy?'

'I will need to leave the band soon.'

The guys go quiet, 'Why?'

'Not that I don't love our skulk rock pioneering. I love it with all my heart.'

'What is it then Jimmy?'

'I have a medical condition.'

Mike Remo's eyes slowly close. Thunderman tries to make light of the announcement,

'Have another beer then!'

'Not that easy TMan.'

The Gnome is constructive, 'We can score something stronger if you like?'

James forces a laugh.

'Well Doctor Charlie has me on a pretty solid program already so I'm feeling ok.'

The Gnome continues, 'What the fuck is the problem Jimmy E?'

Mike Remo opens his eyes. He knows what is looming. He stares at the wall. He doesn't want to look anywhere. His own memories flood back. He feels Stella's hand on his shoulder.

'Well it's known as death!'

'WHAT?'

'Don't make me explain. Please?'

There is silence. Mike digs his nails into his palms and eventually asks, 'How long?'

'Six months tops but a rapid decline to pain and loss of dignity.'

'FuckShitPiss Jimmy!', The MetroGnome looks down at the floor. TMan stares out of the window.

James lightens the mood, or tries to, 'So hey boys we need gigs and recordings as quickly as possible and as many as possible?'

'Fucking right Jimmy!'

'We got to commit to Skulk with more purpose than ever!'

Mike Remo takes a deep deep breath and reaches over and lays a hand on James' head.

'We love you man. That's exactly what we'll do! We start tonight at Ho Far tonight. You feel ok for it?'

'You bet Mike. Dr Charlie has me riding high. I need groove.'

The Dirtkickers all do their best to lift the atmosphere as they load the tour bus for tonight's gig.

The 'Tour Bus' moves into Chinatown with Mike at the wheel. Gigs clear the mind. James gazes out at the dead red chickens hanging in the windows. The crosstown journey is quiet. Even Thunderman is quiet. James finds himself trying to cheer the others up. He asks himself how crazy that is? They pull up outside The Ho Far Bar and a smiling Chinese guy emerges. Mike Remo shakes his hand,

'Ho Chi Minimum! How the fuck are you?'

Ho Chi smiles and responds,

'Sclew you Mike Lemo!'

They hug. Mike Remo sings, 'Hey Ho Hey Ho – we gonna rock and roll.'

Ho smiles, 'Only two sets tonight Big Mike, Big Boss has booked a new band for 3rd and 4th sets!'

'Is there a problem here Ho?'

'No ploblem Mike Lemo, same money for 2 sets! And flee dlinks to compensate?'

'We can use house drum kit too?'

'No ploblem, as long as other band can use your amps?'

Mike looks at James and Thunderman, they nod, 'It's a deal Ho.'

'Many toulists in town Mike. Big Boss wanted 4 sets and late night.'

'That's great Ho. Better for us to have drinking time.'

'I look after you Mike Lemo!'

*

The Dirtkickers quickly set up the stage and move to a quiet corner and get the beers in. They swap stories of past gigs and James smiles and laughs with them.

The bar gradually fills, a mixture of tourists and locals and The Dirtkickers get the sign from Ho. Mike pulls the four of them together,

'Nothing matters but Skulk Rock boys. If they don't get it we don't care. We don't play no covers. We play our tunes. We always do. We make no apologies. We never surrender. Nothing gets in our way. Let's shove some skulk into the space-time continuum. Our job is to put it out there.'

The Lowdown Dirtkickers take the stage.

Mike Remo steps up to the mic, 'This is a song relating to the times in life you come up on situations where there is FUCK ALL you can do! It's called 'Underwater in a locked car – At the bottom of a Reservoir – On a planet so far – Out of orbit round a black star'.'

They look at The Gnome. Mike nods. Three clicks, a snare like a cannon and they are in.

Nothing You Can Do

https://badpeoplethemusical.bandcamp.com/track/nothing-you-can-do

Like you're falling from a thousand miles
Like you lost your teeth and still want to smile
Unconscious pilot in a nose dive
Now you're dead you want to be alive

Nothing you can do
Nothing you can do

Like an outlaw with no alibi

Like a black cloud in a summer sky
Like a witness telling a lie
Or like a gun in the hand of a jealous guy

Nothing you can do
Nothing you can do

Well watch the stars revolve around a nighttime sky
And feel the gravity every time you try to fly
There is nothing you can do

A roulette wheel is bound to lose
I'm telling you all of this bad news
The worst thing is – it's true

You're falling from a thousand miles
No Samaritan you can dial
You're walking down the aisle
And your wedding dress just went out of style

Underwater in a locked car
At the bottom of a reservoir
On a planet so far
Out of orbit round a black star

Nothing you can do
Nothing you can do
There is nothing you can do

The Dirtkickers really go for it. James' news, the beer and the general atmosphere push them along with a groove like never before. James adds a tense solo.

The audience sense it. You can tell when they get it. A light goes on somewhere in the universe and it beams photons through every brain receptor. Tonight Skulk Rock rules the airwaves. The audience draw energy from it. Immense energy. They love it. They want more. The situation makes them thirsty. The bar staff are suddenly occupied. Ho Chi smiles as he has to help behind the bar.

As the song ends applause vibes rule the atmosphere. The dancers want more. There are suddenly more people. The Ho Far Bar is certainly rammed now and as Mike Remo unpacks his saxophone a buzz seems to go around the audience. James looks out over the crowd and spots Felicia and her 3 friends Amanada, Yolande and Miranda enter the bar. As The Dirtkickers groove into the next song they too begin dancing. As usual Felicia commands attention. Her friends are loving it too and dance provocatively with many of the good natured people at the gig.

The whole holy vibe never diminishes. Mike Remo uses every trick he knows. He faces down fate like a fusion bomb. He tells it to 'fuck off'! The audience love him. James watches him work the audience. James loves it too. He smiles at Mike, TMan and The Gnome. He loves these guys. He takes one more of Dr Charlie's tablets during the break. So many people in he can't even get across to speak to Felicia. He smiles over. She waves. The disturbance of the air from her hand reaches him like an affection-tsunami and he is electrified. Ho Chi is loving it. He struggles through the crowd with 2 jugs of beer for the band and places them on the stage. One of his waitresses brings two more. A slim Chinese girl with amazing cheekbones and lined eyebrows that make James' eyes swim along their wavy lines. She smiles at him as he thanks her for the beer. Ho enthuses like never before,

'Mike Lemo you lock! You lock like fuck! Big Boss say I can pay you more tonight!'

'Thanks Ho. We appreciate you giving us gigs. We really do.'

'We buying bigger bar Mike Lemo. It will be Skulk Lock HQ!'

'That's the truth Ho. The whole truth and fuck all but the truth!'

Ho Chi Minimum gives Mike the Skulk Rock salute.

Time hurries. The band could play all night. As the 2nd set approaches the finish the audience calls for more. Mike Remo thanks them and tells them, 'Thank you all Skulk Rockers. We will see you next time. But don't leave. There is another band to play a set in 30 mins or so. How much pleasure can you handle? We need to concentrate on some serious drinking time now.'

Still the audience call for more. Mike Remo calms them down.

'Hey Skulkers, It's well known that this is the best rock bar in SF and Ho Chi has booked another real good band for your entertainment!' He calls over to Ho, 'What are they called Ho?'

'The Snake Blothers. Flom Montana!'

The audience gradually calms. The Dirtkickers move into a rear bar and sit enjoying a drink. They all embrace James. As they sit James asks, 'Hey Mikey, did Ho say The Snake Brothers?'

'No! The Snake Blothers!', Mike laughs at his own joke and hugs James.

'Ha Haaaa. Oh fuck I've heard they are trouble?'

'Never heard of them around here. A bunch of country shit-kickers probably. Anyway they gave us some drinkin time and free drinks. Let's move through to the back bar.'

They struggle through the crowd to a private rear bar that Ho uses as a Green Room. James makes signs across the room to Felicia in order to indicate their destination. She nods. Jugs of beer are waiting for them. The Dirtkickers stand to attention and give each other the Skulk Rock salute. Felicia's smiling face appears around the door frame and she walks in with her three friends. Felicia introduces Amanda, Yolande and Miranda. The Dirtkicker's mood lifts even more. TMan tells The Gnome, 'We're in Babe Basement!' The mood relaxed now as they all sit and share jokes. After a couple of rounds of drinks they hear the next band start up. Crazy as it sounds, the rhythm slithers and menaces. It seems to slide into every corner of the rear bar as if seeking out listeners. It demands attention. Amanda begins to dance in her seat and finally grabs Mike Remo's lapels and teases, 'I neeeeeeed to dance!' The two of them wander through to the main bar just in time to hear King Snake introduce the next song. Amanda looks a bit taken aback by the manifestation of The Snake Brothers. Mike Remo also stops in his tracks for a few moments. The music is hard to categorise. Loose rhythms and a very bass rich sound with a mixture of blues and melodic scales that seem to worm their way into the listener.

All the Snakes seem truly scary. Singer/Frontman Snake is built solid with a thick dark tattooed neck. He has thick curly greased hair, slightly grey from red, swept back and the thick skin around his neck almost looks like some kind of 'hood'. He wrings strident chords from a tobacco sunburst Les Paul guitar. His guitar strap is snakeskin and there is what looks like a large hunting knife sheathed on it. Mike Remo giggles to himself internally and sees him as a King Cobra. Drum Snake is similar except slimmer and taller, his long limbs seem to have extended reach. His 'sound' includes percussion effects that resemble rattlesnake rattles and the are seamlessly incorporated into his grooves. Second Guitar Snake is sturdily built like King Cobra Frontman with thick stubby fingers moving efficiently over his black Les Paul guitar. His overdriven sound seems to place a 'hiss' on the edge of each note he exudes. As he plays, his tongue darts in and out of his mouth. Mike wonders to himself if they worked this 'snakiness' up or whether it is actually how they are. Has evolution played a strange trick here. Missing links of some sort? Bass Snake is different though; she is a slim athletic girl. Her raven black hair hangs in curtains tending to obscure her face from the many gazes that she draws. She plays a black Fender Precision bass. She wears a black leather skirt and black/grey snakeskin jacket. Her long slim fingers are adorned in silver jewelry. Her bass lines are integral to the sound. Unexpected but always grooved. Mike characterises her as more birdlike than reptilian. The spotlights accentuate her collar length black hair and seem to reflect in rainbow colours from the darkness. She is a raptor for sure. She draws his eyes.

The frontman introduces himself as 'King' Snake in a voice that is both grunt and hiss. The audience are shocked into some kind of trance already. His manner is ugly. His words chosen to alarm. Whether by design or by nature King snake and his 'band' create a negative tension. The rhythms are seductive but the tension is inhibiting. The audience want to dance but only the drunken-most are left in gyration. Most of the audience stand and watch. Mike notices how strange that an electric atmosphere of good will can change into negative charge so quickly.

King snake makes a strange gesticulation to the audience as if to mesmerise them. His hand raising slowly upwards like a snake's head. He rings some boogie chords from his Les Paul.

Hypnosis

https://badpeoplethemusical.bandcamp.com/track/hypnosis

It's takin place – In a purple haze
Listen to what I say – As you drift away
Watch my swinging gold watch – You're gonna like it a lot
I'm taking control – Of your body and soul

I was a superhero – but I quit
I was a hitman – 'til I got hit
Now I'm a mind reader – I got your mind and I'm lookin at it
You can't resist
You know you can't resist
No woman can resist
My hypnosis

So you can relax – You know I'm gonna bring you back
I will count to ten – Snap my fingers and thenn
You will feel secure – No worries anymore
The future is my design – No point in you tryin...

To resist
This is how it is
Looking into an abyss
It's hypnosis

I was a superhero – but I quit
I was a hitman – 'til I got hit
Now I'm a mind reader – I got your mind and I'm lookin at it
You can't resist
You know you can't resist
No woman can resist
My hypnosis

You are feeling sleepy,
I know I'm sounding creepy

But I hope you understand   That I am in command
You are in safe hands
I got no evil plans
It's hypnosis
It's just hypnosis

Mike Remo and Amanda are the only people dancing now; Mike
is hardened to these atmospheres and Amanda is buzzing on wine
and whatever else. Mike smiles at her but knows that women like
Amanda won't stick around. Nevertheless, he likes her and is
enjoying her temporary attachment to him. The song grooves but

somehow The Snake Brothers seem to exude too much menace. Amanda sinks into the music and is swept along; she begins to enjoy being on display. Someone in the crowd distracts Mike and he steps over to chat as Amanda continues to dance alone for now.

Noticing her dancing alone, Second Guitar Snake steps down from the stage and gyrates with Amanda as he riffs his guitar. As the song finishes he leans forward with a leary whisper into Amanda's ear. Amanda looks shocked and pushes him away. He moves to walk away but, as if by a considered response, he turns and head butts Amanda who immediately goes to the floor. The room gasps and Mike Remo turns around and sees Amanda on the floor with her nose smashed and bleeding.

The audience are quiet and in shock. Mike Remo looks at the stage, 'What the fuck?' The audience fall silent. Yolanda and Miranda appear and help Amanda to her feet.

King Cobra Snake now moves forward, looking directly at Mike Remo, hissing and grunting into the mic, 'Do you want the same shit city boy? Because, if you do, stick around. Otherwise, take your city ass and your city tart and fuck right on off into the night.'

Mike Remo calmly looks at King Snake, not moving an inch. From nowhere he pulls a handgun and shoots. The shot is followed by a loud overdriven dischord. King Snake staggers and looks down at his guitar.

Mike has shot his guitar and the slug is embedded in the maple capped mahogany body. Everybody is stunned. Mike Remo breaks the silence,

'I always wondered if a Gibson Les Paul in Tobacco Sunburst would stop a bullet?'

As King Snake steps forward now Mike stares him down, 'Good job you don't play an SG fat overgrown bullhead piece of shit country boy. Will your gut smother a bullet?'

King snake shows no sign of backing down and now has the large knife from his guitar strap in his hand. There is tense silence until a loud shotgun blast shatters it and the ceiling plaster above King Snake's head. Dust and debris falls down onto and all around King Snake. Ho Chi steps forward with a Winchester Pump in his hands,

'Get the fuck out of my bar you countly plick.'

King Snake looks momentarily stunned. He is now surrounded by Ho's smartly suited doormen. After some thought however, he sees the sense in Ho's suggestion. The Snakes unplug their instruments and slowly leave the bar walking past Amanda receiving attention from Felicia and her friends.

As the dust settles and Mike Remo walks over to the girls.

James sits in a corner alone now, staring ahead. His face pale in a moonlight beam through the bar skylight. He looks like a ghost.

Speed Gun

James walks through a misty San Francisco morning. He takes in some views and sings to himself. As he walks across Haight a female traffic cop manifests herself from a concealed doorway. She seems somehow full of life and energy. She is not inhibited by people on the street as she points an electronic device at a high revving sports car with an impatient driver.

She speaks to herself as James passes, 'Sonoffabitch!'

'Did you get him?'

The cop turns and smiles enthusiastically, 'He's been hit by a speed gun!'

'You a good shot with that thing?'

'I never miss. I'm the grim reaper of speed.'

She points the speed gun at James and makes a gun/ricochet sound and then 'blows across the barrel' in a mimic western style. She smiles at James, 'You better not speed around while I'm in town!'

Her countenance is irrepressible and James can't help but smile. He thinks to himself that in different circumstances he would stop and talk to her. Maybe even get to buy her a drink when she is off duty. Maybe even get to fall in love with her. Maybe even get her to wear her uniform in private for him. He'd take a taser for her for sure. Somehow though, his present condition doesn't seem to allow him that freedom. He tries to say all that to her in a smile and he thinks she gets it. Telepathy is a wonderful talent that he has. She has it too. Their instant love affair cheers him as he steals himself the energy to walk up the hill to Ronee and Lucy's flat door. He rings the bell and a Hendrix riff sounds. Lucy answers the door wrapped in a blanket and looking sleepy.

'It's you!'

'Yup. Can I come in?'

'Spose.'

'Had a heavy night?'

'I had a gig over in Oakland. Late back.'

'How'd it go?'

'Good, real good.'

She makes him coffee as he looks out over the rooftops.

'Hey Lucy, where's your guitar?'

From the kitchen. 'Next to my bed.'

James picks up the guitar and hits a few chords. He sings, 'Time is upon me like a pack of wolves, Graviteeeee like an avalanche …'

Lucy appears from the kitchen, 'And I got sins I can't absolve, just like everyone!'

They smile and both say together, 'It's a keeper!'

Lucy produces a pad and a pencil.

James adds, 'Got a chorus start', he messes with chords, 'I been hit by a speed gun, Time is a policewoman', Lucy adds,'We're all on the run, The bitch is after everyone.'

They laugh as they write it down.

'Let's give it some class with a key change?'

'Let's give it two!'

'Yeh man!'

James and Lucy are lost in a song creation whirlwind. The clouds pass by outside. They pass the guitar.

Eventually James sings this song alone to Lucy.

Lucy smiles as if the song were a new child born to them.

Speed Gun

https://badpeoplethemusical.bandcamp.com/track/speed-gun

Time is upon me like a pack of wolves
Gravity like an avalanche
These are problems I can't solve
And I'm not the only one

Cinema in the back of my mind
Keeps replaying all of my crimes
Memories malinger
Like death's cold finger

I been hit by a speed gun
Time is a – policewoman
We're all on the run
The bitch is after everyone
Time bomb – time bomb – time bomb
Weapon of mass destruction
Fall asleep and you wake up
Fall asleep and you wake up
Fall asleep and you wake up gone

All of your memories – erased for good
By time's fell hand defaced –
In cold cold blood
I wouldn't bullshit you
Everything I say is true .
And I'm not even tellin you
The lies you want to hear?

How did I ever get in this condition?
The last thing I remember was the foetal position
In a care home waitin' to die
I can still hear My Mother's lullabye

I don't think of that – just you
Our time bomb was for two
We can still escape
Better not leave it too late

We been hit by a speed gun – speed gun
Time is a – policewoman
We're all on the run
They are after everyone
Time bomb – time bomb – time bomb
It's a big explosion
Weapon of mass destruction
Fall asleep and you wake up
Fall asleep and you wake up
Fall asleep and you wake up gone

'Hey Jimmy, that's a good song!'

'It's our song Lucy?'

'Well Jimmy, the ideas were yours.'

'Wish they weren't!'

'Don't say that Jimmy. You have a keeper there!'

'It's the only song I ever made up that has any truth in it Lucy?'

'I don't understand?'

'Well, mostly my songs are bullshit items!'

Lucy laughs, 'And this isn't?'

'Nope!'

'You mean you got a speeding ticket?'

'From the doctor. Yes!'

Lucy partly realises his meaning now and asks, 'What's the problem Jimmy Smith?'

'3 months.'

'3 MONTHS? You're not making sense?'

'6 months 3 months. It's how long I got?'

Lucy is shocked. Her eyes fill with tears. Silence besieges the room and then invades. Eventually, James tries to be jovial. He fails miserably.

'Who gives a shit? We all got to go sometime?'

'I give a shit. I'm pregnant.'

Silence takes control once more. Neither of them says anything now as they run all the cliché conversations in their minds. Eventually Lucy walks over to him and they embrace.

Lucy begins to sing (Smith's tune), 'What a mess I've made of my life … '

James replies, 'No justice. Is there?'

'Well we are bad people James. Looks like what goes around comes around? It should be me who is terminal!'

'We're all terminal Lucy. Just wish it wasn't so close.'

'We need a Sydney Carton!'

'We sure do.'

'Do you know any Mr Darnay?'

They stare from the window. Neither of them emotional. James muses, 'Fucking tough to make a living out of music?'

He pauses, then, 'Hey Lucy. Don't want to panic you so stay calm. The Snake Brothers turned up at Ho Chi's Bar last night!'

Lucy staggers, she turns pale, a black cloud passes over the sun and the shadow weaves into the room. She moves away from the window and actually cowers in the corner; she sinks down to her haunches, 'You didn't think to tell me?'

'I just told you!'

She bursts into tears. James comforts, 'We can sort this out.'

Through tears, 'How the FUCK can I sort this out? Kill them all?'

They look at each other and manage a laugh.

Lucy looks thoughtful, 'Guess I'll have to move again? FUCK! I love it around here.'

James thinks, 'Maybe I CAN be Sydney Carton?'

'You mean you'll confess to killing Seth and take my rap?'

'Wouldn't work Lucy.'

She musters a laugh, 'C'mon Jimmy English do the decent thing!'

There's another silence before Lucy adds, 'Guess I could kill them all?'

'Wouldn't work Lucy!'

'Oh listen to Mr FuckinItFuckinWouldn'tFuckinWork. Why wouldn't it work? I'm already a killer.'

'So am I!'

Lucy stares at him incredulously, 'How so Public Enemy Number 1? Don't tell me you still think you killed your Dad?'

'I did.'

'You fuckin didn't. You had an argument and – ok – used a bad word? You never saw him again?

Hardly a case of ulta-violence?'

James stares.

Lucy descends into sarcasm, 'killing someone properly needs some kind of weapon? Don't tell me you are trained in a verbal martial art and your words are officially weapons?'

James enters the sarcasm war with an irony torpedoe, 'Well, such is the power of my poetry I can reduce living beings to rotting carcasses with carefully chosen wordbolts.'

Now James is tearful and she regains some self-awareness, 'So get over it you lily-livered limey.'

He looks at Lucy for some kind of understanding. She stares

back and James continues, 'He took my guitar and smashed it!'

We see Lucy's face and tears roll down her cheeks, 'Yesssss James, you told me.'

Unexpectedly Lucy holds him.

James carries on, 'I left home right after and came to the US. He died 6 months later.'

Lucy calmly replies, 'Yes you told me', she let's James go on, 'He recovered physically but Mum said he was never the same. Maybe we both got the same 'condition'? Maybe fate's way of telling us to behave?'

'Deliberately breaking guitars is still a capital offence Jimmy E!', she just about manages joviality.

'Fate should fucking understand that civilised people no longer accept the death penalty as any part of a justice system? If we did should kill Pete Townshend while we're at it?'

Now they are both in tears. James tells her again how his father loved old musicals. He's told her before but she lets him continue to ramble, 'Sad thing is my Dad actually loved music and I grew up listening to him playing LP Records of musicals. He loved the old musicals. Carousel was his fave. I think he kind of thought that you had to be from an aristocratic trained background to work in music? Maybe that's true and Skulk Rock is never going to dominate the arts?'

There's a silence. Lucy holds him then she softly sings, 'If I loved you, words wouldn't come in an easy way …'

James responds by singing some of Billy Bigelow's lines,

> You can't hear a sound, not the turn of a leaf
> Nor the fall of a wave hittin' the sand.
> The tide's creepin' up on the beach like a thief,
> Afraid to be caught stealin' the land!
> On a night like this I start to wonder
> What life is all about?

'We don't know what love is about either do we Jimmy Smith?'

'Love is looking after kids Lucy Smith! All that's left of us is love.'

Eventually, 'Well looks like we need a Sydney Carton AND a Billy Bigelow?'

'Or, more realistically, maybe I'd better just leave town?'

'NO. Leave it with me Lucy and I will sort this shit out!'

As they embrace two ravens circle outside the window, their blackness like shadows across the blue sky now.

18

Hound Dog Man

James lies in bed one Monday morning. He listens to the city sounds drifting across rooftops and up the hill to his flat. He watches a disc of light progress across the wall, plotting its arc in his mind. It reminds him of his bedroom at home. He kills those thoughts and gets out of bed. He makes himself a pot of tea and goes through the ceremony of Doctor Charlie's medicines. He hears a Harley outside followed by an irregular thumping on the door a few flights of stairs below. As he negotiates the stairs, he is reminded of the old 'drummer at the door' joke. He giggles as he remembers trying to use that joke on The Gnome one time. The Gnome had asked him,

'What's the difference between a gynaecologist and a drummer?'

His answer being, 'A gynaecologist only works with one cunt at a time!' Followed by The Gnome dance.

He opens the door to the spectacle of Marv in full Angel regalia, complete with red bandana. James blurts,

'I got the $1400 Marv! I just haven't had chance to bring it over!'

Marv smiles, 'No worries James English', in his faux English accent. James laughs. Marv continues, 'But a coffee would be nice.'

Marv follows James upstairs and gazes from the window until James produces the coffee. As Marv sits he produces a hip flask and adds some liquor to his coffee. He offers it to James who figures it might be polite not to refuse. Marv does the honours.

'Michael Remo tells me you had some trouble with those Snake-fuckers the other night?'

'We surely did Marv. Mike pulled a gun!'

'His Ma always took a gun to gigs. Looks like she trained young Michael well too? You can never be too careful?'

Marv sips his coffee and makes a 'chaaaaaaa' sound of satisfaction.

'Thing is Jimmy E, you can forget the $1400. We can call it quits if you can do a little job for me and Don?'

James is somewhat relieved as he isn't quite sure he can lay his hands on $1400 without asking Mike for help. He smiles, 'Sure thing Marv.'

'We don't like those Snakefuckers one little bit either and we need to get a tracker on to their vehicle so we can locate their whereabouts?'

James nods.

'We figured you might know the places they might be playing and could find an opportunity to deploy a tracker for us.'

Marv produces a small device with a magnetic base. He walks over and sticks it to James' fridge.

'I'd be happy to Marv. But what is your interest?'

'They behaved in a threatening manner to us. Big mistake Jimmy! Don is worried they might find out where little Lucy lives and she lives with Ronee. And, you know Ronee is Don's daughter?'

'I didn't know that Marv.'

'We would just be happier if we knew where they were. Bringing up kids is tricky for me and Don.'

James nods again, 'I'd love to help Marv. I need to know where they are too!'

Marv smiles, 'Marv's Motors have the technology Jimmy.'

He looks out of the window, 'Nice view Jimmy E. Nice day for a ride out to Marin. Let me know?'

James nods again and they shake hands. He feels honoured somehow to be given a task by Marv. Not to mention the cancellation of his debt.

As he returns upstairs and looks in his various underground music press mags. He speaks to himself,

'OK Mr King Snake, where are you sons of bitches playing tonight?', he spots an ad, 'ah-ha Mad Lennie's Bar!'

James thinks to himself what a nightmare gig that will be? Mike Remo hates the place and won't play there. Too much tension, too much anger and minimal security. San Francisco's underground hard punk, death metal and trip groove scene. It's a nightmare for drugs and violence.

'Best place for The Snakes though!', James muses to himself, 'Maybe they'll get massacred?'

As the night of The Snakes gig falls James sits in the dirtkicker van outside Mad Lennie's Bar. The clientele spill onto the streets. Some fight, some stagger, some puke and some pass out. James watches impassively. Two younger guys stagger past and he exits the van, 'Who's playing there tonight guys?'

'The Snakemen or something. Wild night. Too much for us!'

'Have they finished?'

'Nah, there's another set yet. Too crazy for us!'

James climbs back into the van and waits until he hears the set start. He recognizes the bass lines escaping the building fabric. It's later and the surroundings are otherwise quiet. All clientele has moved back into the venue. He picks up Marv's tracker. He walks around the venue to the car park and loading bays. He sees the SnakeTruck, as described by Marv parked close by a two storey brick wall. He checks no-one is around and quickly lies on his back, attaching the tracker device to a structural chassis member. He checks it is stable and safe. As he carefully rolls out from under the vehicle he hears a faint fluttering noise. He stands now and looks around with his back to the truck. He is relieved no-one is around assuming the noise to have been the breeze blowing something around. As he turns he staggers in shock as he looks up to see a bird the size of turkey perched on the rear of the snaketruck. He staggers back and stumbles over a kerbed walkway and ends up on his back. He now realises that the bird is no turkey as it opens a vast wingspan and floats to the ground. He thinks to himself, 'It's a fucking eagle?' His mind panics. The eagle bends his head under the truck as if to see what James has been doing. The bird then walks slowly towards James who is frozen. It turns its head to one side and stares. He feels like it is staring into his mind. The eagle now turns and runs two or three steps before becoming airborne.

James shakes as he regains his feet and trembles his way back to the parked Dirtkicker van. In the van he shakes as his composure slowly returns. He takes a Doctor Charlie.

In time the bass groove stops and clientele begin to spill out of the club. They mill around, slowly disappearing into the night. Eventually he sees King Snake standing on the sidewalk outside the venue. There is a full moon over his head and his aura reaches out scarily. James watches impassively from the van. He watches the other Snakes appear as they load instrumennts back into the van. Eventually there is a deep throated diesel sound as The Snake Truck starts and moves around to the front of the club. The tall slim figure of the bass player appears from a rear door as King Snake wanders back into the club. James notices how slim and attractive she is stood under the moonlight. A few minutes later King Snake reappears from the club and climbs into the Snaketruck. It moves off. James grips the steering wheel of the Dirtkicker van with white knuckles now as he follows the snake truck. It travels out of town west towards the ocean.

Hound Dog Man

https://badpeoplethemusical.bandcamp.com/track/hound-dog-man

There was a tear in my eye – but it long since dried
I said goodbye – but it was a lie
Hear me howl like a wolf – a wolf in the night 7
Hound dog dreams never turn out right

They look for me – but I can't be found
They want me gone – but I'm still around
My hound dog heart beats with no sound
I bury my hound dog bones – deep underground

I'm a hound dog – I'm a hound dog man
I'm comin for you – Just as fast as I can
I'm a hound dog – I'm a hound dog man
I'm comin for you – Just as fast as I can

I follow rivers and drink from lakes
I watch and I wait – until I get my break
I'm always on the take
I got a million dollars to make
Ice turning black no turnin back on this highway
This is no place for a cry baby
Fate is a gambler – he will deal your hand
You always need an alternative plan

Cos I'm a hound dog – I'm a hound dog man

I'm comin for you – Just as fast as I can
But I'm a hound dog – I'm a hound dog man
I'm comin for you – Just as fast as I can

So I'm steppin off a plane In your neighbourhood
I find my way Through the darkest wood
So I'm on a ship The stars are looking good
I'm on your scent I can smell your blood

I'm a hound dog – I'm a hound dog man
I'm comin for you – Just as fast as I can
I'm a hound dog – I'm a hound dog man
I'm comin for you – Just as fast as I can

He follows at a distance until the SnakeTruck pulls into a high fenced rental property. James pulls off the highway nearby and makes full note of the location.

It's a clear night now and the drug regime Dr Charlie has him on tends to keep him wired. He should never have taken the extra dose and he mentally blames the eagle. He decides to look out over the ocean once again as it is nearby. He gets back on the highway and heads west. As he cruises the coastal highway heading south he sees a 'viewpoint' sign and turns down an access road. The road leads him to a secluded car park with the ocean laid out in front of him. The moon hovers and stars are visible. James gets out of the van and the sound of the rollers breaking obscures the noise of any traffic on the nearby highway. As he turns around he sees a steep drop to the beach below, probably about 50 feet. He looks at the drop and notices sail boats parked on the beach below. He wonders how you would get a boat down there and notices a zig zag ramp at the far end of the viewpoint parking area. A tractor is parked nearby. Looking to his left a dirt road runs steeply upwards behind a row of poplar trees to some rough agricultural land. He wonders to himself how long it will be before that is developed for yet another coast side resort. He walks over and looks at the land. As he walks back to the Dirtkicker van a plan begins to form in his mind …

The following day finds James driving The Dog cross town and pulling into Marv' Motors once again.

Marv looks out from the workshop and walks out half glaring half staring at James,

'Fuck me Jimmy E. Thought I'd seen the back of this old 'Dawg'.'

'Hey Marv. I deployed the tracker but I got another problem.'

James tells Marv selected details of The Snake problem. He tells him that circumstances have changed and Lucy is pregnant.

'Congratulations Jimmy English we heard you are always falling in lerv! Now you will find out about the associated problems.'

James laughs but now tells Marv he needs rid of The Snakes once and for all. Marv is now a little more edgy.

'I don't know any hit men Jimmy E. Maybe, just maybe, you might tell the 'authoriteeeeees'?'

'An angel telling me that?'

Marv laughs, 'That's right The Mascara Snake – fast and bulbous'.

'Bulbous also tapered'.

'Also a tin teardrop'!

They both laugh at the Captain Beefheart quotes until James turns serious, 'Marv I'm gonna ram the shit out of them!'

Marv laughs, 'Whatever?', James continues,

'I need an edge though. Can you fit me a supersafe and shock resistant driver seat into The Dog?'

Marv looks vacantlyand puzzled at him.

'Please Marv, I'm serious here!'

Marv seems annoyed now rubbing his chin, 'You wanna waste your time and money on crazy schemes Jim, I'll take your money. I can put a drag racer's bucket seat in there and shock mount it for you. 250 bucks. Come back in 2 days!'

James realises Marv wants the conversation over. He confirms his requirements and counts out the money.

James walks out of the yard and Marv watches him go, shaking his head.

James is floating now as he crosses town. His thoughts blur and whirl. He thinks of Lucy and worries about how he left her tense by mentioning The Snakes. He hopes she hasn't done anything crazy like left town. The worry builds in his mind and he panic-rushes over to the house. As he rings the door chime there is no reply.

He shouts through the letter box now. Eventually the door slowly opens and Lucy's nervous face smiles at him. As she invites him in he sees her rucksack in the centre of the room and the Nick Lucas case nearby.

'Lucy you can't leave town!'

'I have to!'

'NO, I'm going to sort this out.'

She holds him, 'You can't, it's not your problem is it?'

'Yes it is my problem!. It's our child isn't it?'

'Yes, it must be!'

They fall silent and Lucy makes coffee. As James sits on the couch now he moves a box to one side and notices its weight. Curiosity makes him lift off the top and he sees Howard's gun in there and the ammunition. As Lucy returns she sees him looking at the contents,

'It was a gift!'

James looks open mouthed, 'Hey LuLu we don't want to do anything stupid here!'

'You're the one being stupid thinking you can 'negotiate' with The Snakes.'

'I have a plan.'

Lucy looks at him and shakes her head, 'There's nothing you can do James. NOTHING!'

He stares back with madness in his eyes, 'Give me a few more days?'

Her emotions take over and her tears flow. She collapses on the couch beside him. James holds her. Maybe it's Doctor Charlie's treatment plan or maybe the circumstances or maybe both but his mind brings everything into sharp focus now. It must generate a confident tone in his voice because she calms down and agrees,

'You won't do anything stupid then Jimmy Smith?'

'Of course not. Could I borrow your gun?'

She turns in fake shock now. They both laugh.

'I really do have a plan Lucy!'

She nods in implicit agreement. Together they work out how to load the gun. As James slots in the last cartridge and clicks the barrel closed

'We're children in a grown-up's world here James Smith, and it's grown-ups who have fucked this world!'

'We're bad people Lucy Smith!'

19

Park and Ride

Marv has the dragster bucket seat in the middle of the yard as Don rides in on his Harley 'Fat Boy.'

'What's goin on Marv?'

'You wouldn't believe me.'

'Try me.'

He attaches the seat to a steel frame with resilient shock mounts. Don walks around the job, 'Not another drag racer Marv?'

'Nope, young Jimmy English from The Dirtkickers says he is gonna ram the crap out of the Snakefuckers?'

'What?'

'Oh yeh man. He reckons he needs rid of them. Says he's gonna ram them and needs a safety seat in his truck.'

'Well, I suppose it would solve our problems?'

'Not sure it would solve his? He seems a little different these days?'

Marv and Don both seem puzzled and laugh, 'He's not your average stoner?'

'He tells me his little girlfriend Lucy is gonna have to leave town if he don't get these guys offof her back.'

'Awwww, he's in love again?'

'Sounds like it. Mike Remo says he is a sucker for the women! Dumb limey. I dunno though he is a good kid?'

Marv bolts up the resilient shock mounts and wobbles the seat in the frame to check everything. Don helps. They work well together.

'You know what Marv. I kinda like that little Lucy?'

'Reckon so. Mike Remo has got her onto the music circuit that's how English Jimmy met her.'

'There's something else going on here Marv.'

'Right. He did tell me he'd fitted that tracker.'

'Daughters Marv, you gotta love 'em but they are a worry all your life.'

'Goddam right. Maybe we'd better keep a good eye on this situation?'

Don and Marv work together fitting the seat and frame into The Dog. It's an ugly fit with visible boltwork out of the roof but it seems to work well as Marv tests it with a few emergency stops around the yard. On Don's suggestion they also weld on a heavy set of bull bars to the front.

*

Across town James meets Felicia once more in Boudins. The electricity gone from their secret liaison.

'Rich is out of town for a week or so.'

'How is Amanda?'

'Broken nose, got reset. She has good cover.'

'I'm so sorry.'

'She lost one of her modelling contracts.'

James repeats, 'So so sorry.'

Pause.

'Not your fault Jimmy E. Who were those guys? I hate them!'

'Long story Fil. I need to deal with them. Could use your help?'

'Count me in Jimmy E. I need an adventure.'

'Could be this Friday when they have a gig over at Fisherman's Wharf.'

'And your plan is?' …

*

James arrives back at Marv's Motors later that day. He is absorbed in his circumstances. Tunnel vision as he stares straight ahead walking into Marv's office. Marv and Don are in an embrace and James does not even notice he is so lost in thought.

'Don't you fuckin limeys ever knock?'

James apologises. Marv laughs and the three of them walk out to where The Dog sits in the yard.

'We put some crash bars on the front there. Thought it might be useful?'

'Oh wow, never thought of that. Do I owe you?'

'On the house Jimmy E.'

James tries the seat. Marv and Don look at each other with

puzzled expressions. Marv asks, 'When is your big hit taking place Jimmy E?'

James is a little lost in thought as he struggles with the pilot style safety harness.

'Their next gig will be their last!'

'Where's that?'

'GigCity on the Wharf.'

Marv and Don smile at each other. Don asks one last question, 'Hey Jimmy, those snake guys don't know where your little girl-friend lives do they?'

'No and they never will.'

Marv and Don look at each other unconvinced as James drives out of the yard.

*

As the evening of the gig arrives James parks The Dog on the street just along from the GigCity venue. He walks up to the venue and hears the muffled SnakeRock from within. He thinks to himself, 'Love those bass lines.' A guy staggers out of the venue with blood pouring from his nose. James asks the doorman what time the gig is due to end. He goes back to sit in The Dog. An hour or so later Felicia's Porsche pulls up behind him. Felicia has changed her hair and outfit and looks her usual stunning self, if a little different. She looks just a little too overtly sexy in James' opinion.

'Don't worry Jimmy E. I do know how to pull dumb guys as well as rich guys!', she giggles although James detects she is nervous too.

'You do know where you've got to bring them Fil?'

'Of course. You showed me.'

'Any problems bale out. If you're not there by 2:45am abort the mission.'

'Acknowledge, Affirmative, Roger, Over and Out!', she jokes

James looks at his watch, 'It's about time?' He kisses her on the cheek and, confidently, she descends from the truck and walks to the venue. James sighs as he watches her walk (like only Felicia can walk). He sees her walk to the GigCity entrance and enter. The doorguy can't help himself look her up and down. She enters the gig, buys wine and works her way to the front. As she emerges from the front of the mosh Jake Snake immediately stares at her. Felicia stares back and Jake is the one to look away first. His guttural hissy patter over the mic seems to command a silence now,

'This is our last groove for tonight. You CityBillyMotherFuckers don't pay enough for any encores. You been 'snaked'!'

He looks at Felicia once again, 'If'n you want more snaking you're welcome.' His eyes narrow and his tongue darts in and out. Felicia shivers but doesn't let it show. King Snake continues. 'This one is called Park and Ride.' His black eyes seem to burrow into her mind before Sly Snake drumlicks the song into life.

Park and Ride

https://badpeoplethemusical.bandcamp.com/track/park-and-ride

Why don't you and I try park and ride
All you gotta do is step outside
Come and see what I got
It's waiting outside in the parking lot

I got a line laid out on the dash
You got time and I got cash
Baby, you got that touch of class
You are a fine piece of ass

Why don't we try – park and ride
Time is never on your side
How do you know if you never tried?
Why don't you and I try park and ride

I run a Gold Buick Six
I like to ride and I need my fix
My bullshit – is bonafide
I'm the only prophet who never lied

Why don't we try – park and ride
Time is never on your side
How do you know if you never tried?
Why don't you and I try park and ride

When I got my black Cadillac
I told my Daddy I'm not comin back

There's a highway right outside
The stars will be my guide

Why don't we try – park and ride
Time is never on your side
How do you know if you never tried
Why don't you and I try park and ride

As the rhythm kicks in, the audience start to groove. The Snake Brothers have quickly built a following. The audience have a 'snake dance'. Stoners, pissheads musos all enter the spirit. Felicia joins but doesn't join. Her charisma can look after itself.

Jake Snake keeps staring at Felicia. He can't resist. She holds his gaze as she sways to the music. He plays a guitar break without losing the eyelock he has on her. She keeps cool and her aura matches his. Inwardly she struggles swearing at him beneath her breath. Her skin crawls and she wonders if she is turning into a snake herself. She fights his mental probing until the end of the song.

As the song ends in crescendo, Jake Snake launches himself from the stage and lands with the precision of a gymnast directly in front of Felicia. Still she stares him out. The audience silent and watching by now. Jake seems to expand the loose skin behind his neck, hisses and his tongue darting in and out. As he stops Felicia leans forward and whispers, 'I know the perfect place to park and ride. I can show you if you're outside and ready to roll in thirty minutes?'

She turns and melts into the crowd. King scans the mosh and sees her disappear through one of the exits. He turns and tells Sly, Si and AJ to pack up quick, 'fucking quick!' Jake explains, 'The bitch in the mosh wants snaking and King Snake is on the case.'

King finds the promoter and picks up the $1400 they had agreed. The promoter tries to shake his hand but King ignores him.

'Next time the price is $2000!'

The promoter nods. King adds, '$3000 if you want to spend time with AJ on bass?'

The promoter laughs but King just stares. 'Think about it! Sssssssssssssss!'

The Snakes quickly pack up their equipment and pack it into the truck. As King checks his watch he drives slowly out of the parking lot scanning the street. He suddenly spots Felicia waiting in her open top Porsche parked on the street. She pauses to give a wave. The Snakes 'whoop' and sing Park and Ride in the snake truck as they follow. Jake Snake grips the steering wheel tightly locked in concentration. Felicia alternates her speed.

Sly Snake warns, 'The bitch is winding you up Pa!'

'No boy. She's hot for it. Believe me!', he shakes his head and flaps the loose skin behind his neck.

'Pa, she could take us miles out of our way?'

'I don't care. I'm hot tonight!'

Si Snake shouts excitedly from the back, 'Can I go in after you Pa?'

'You could boy but I'm going to destroy her!'

In the back AJ looks up with a frown. Si asks, 'Really destroy her pa?'

'Enough that she remembers the experience forever boy!'

Si lets out a hisswhistle. 'Make it permanent Pa?' Sly looks across and hisses too, 'Yeh!'

The three of them focussed now. AJ shrinks into her seat in the back. She's never seen them this bad. As the truck reaches an elevated highway she gazes out of the window to her right. The moon hangs low and she sees an eagle against its disc of silver light. The speed of the eagle seems to match theirs such that it stays over the moon disc. She mutters to herself, 'Ooljee, Ajei, Atsah' (In Assiniboine, her mother's name, her name and great eagle). The eagle looks over at her.

James reaches the viewpoint car park and is relieved it is deserted. He carefully backs The Dog about one hundred yards up the dirt track undercover of the poplar trees. He is strapped in to the pilot seat Marv has welded into the Dog Truck. He looks at his watch. He keeps the engine running. He takes one of the pills Doctor Charlie has given him. Moonlight reflects over the water. The breakers crash in with a regularity tonight. There is not much wind but there must have been a storm miles out in the ocean? He thinks of Lucy and her stories about the moon. He looks at his watch, it's 2:35 now. He worries about Felicia. He worries about his plan. He checks his safety harness clips. He checks the safety strap Marv has fitted to restrain his forehead. His heart beats out a fast shuffle rhythm; the breaking waves like crash cymbals accentuating his thoughts. Could this really work? Doubts crawled into his mind now. Too late to stop now (wasn't that a Van Morrison album?). His fingers cramp as he tightgrips The Dog steering wheel. He keeps the engine ticking over.

On the coastal highway now. Felicia keeps her speed to regulation 55mph. She keeps a vigil on the SnakeTruck behind. It stays a steady 30 yards behind.

Sly Snake watches her intently from the passenger seat, 'Don't lose her Pa!'

He looks over at Jake Snake and two veins bulge on his moonlit forehead as Felicia reaches the sign for the viewpoint. Jake laughs, 'This is so convenient. Not a long drive home after she's dogmeat'.

'You gonna be tired Pa?'

Si snake is excited now, 'Bet her husband bought her that car too?'

'You bet he did boy!'

'We gonna show her how to keep a man sat-isssss-fieddddd!'

Felicia rounds a final corner and slows. She turns into the viewpoint about 50 yards ahead of the Snake Truck. As she halts the car she looks to her right and sees the row of poplar trees. She adjusts her parking position forward by a few yards and looks in her mirror; exactly where she and James had planned.

James sees her headlights coming down the access road and revs The Dog ready. He fastens the restraint around his forehead. He sees The SnakeTruck behind her. His mind buzzes. The Doctor's pills work just fine. His thoughts clear as the moon now. He accelerates. He hits 50mph as The SnakeTruck pulls up behind Felicia.

Jake Snake's window is down but he doesn't hear The Dog screaming down the hill because of the sound of the ocean rollers breaking on the moonlit sand 50 feet below. Jake sees Felicia turn her head and tells Sly, 'She's mine now boy. Told you she wanted snaking!' As he turns to open the door it's too late.

James hits 60mph as he switches on the headlights. He sees King Snake turn his big head. Time seems to freeze as he sees King Snakes eyes narrow and his tongue dart. James must be 6 feet from

King Snake at impact. He doesn't remember much else other than opening his eyes as he slams backwards and forwards in Marv's safety seat. The Dog has stopped dead at impact. As he focusses he sees the SnakeTruck catapult to the cliff edge. It is almost stopped by a row of low rocks that tourists can sit on looking out to sea. It teeters and then rolls over and out of sight and down the cliff. Amazingly The Dog's lights still work and their beams shine over the cliff and out to sea.

The Dog Truck is oscillating back and forth on its suspension and The Snake Truck has disappeared into the void; a dustcloud all that remains. Felicia, out of the Porsche now, walks forward to the edge just in time to see the Snake Truck bounce down the rocks and onto the beach. She watches for a while before turning and looking at The Dog Truck. James sits in the pilot seat looking shocked. Felicia looks in through his window.

'You ok Jimmy E?'

'Think so.'

'Mission accomplished?'

'Looks that way!'

'It's put Snake Rock back by 10 years!'

'It is history Felicia.'

'So are we Jimmy E. We better be gone!'

'Are you ok Felicia?'

'Yeh. Not the first guys I killed!'

James looks a little surprised.

'But don't worry. I love you!', she walks forward and kisses him.

As she walks away she turns, 'We're bad people. Aren't we?'

Before James can formulate a reply the Porsche is disappearing away up towards the highway. He manoeuvres The Dog into a parking position and switches the lights off. He feels some kind of relief as the thought of telling Lucy he has solved her problems begins to circulate in his mind. Now he walks forward and looks over the cliff edge. The SnakeTruck is upside down on the beach, steam rising from it. As he stares a shadow crosses the moon and he looks up to see the eagle. It takes his eye as it glides slowly downwards zig-zagging as if checking for a safe landing. It lands on a rock near the truck and as James looks in amazement at it his eyes discern a movement from one of the truck doors thrown open. He looks more closely, blinking to try and improve his vision. His heart thumps like a kick drum through a reflex bass cabinet. He senses panic rising. He looks one way and then the other. He now remembers Lucy's gun and walks quickly over to The Dog. He looks on the seat where he had left it and is shocked to find it gone. His mind jolts before he realises it must have been thrown forward in the impact. He finds the gun in the passenger side footwell and a scattering of shells around it. He picks up the gun and walks to the cliff edge again. Two figures are now visible crawling from the wrecked truck below. He walks quickly to the path beside the access ramp and begins to descend to the beach below.

The path leads to the beach about 50 yards south of where the SnakeTruck has landed. James cocks the pistol and slowly walks towards the upturned truck. As he walks he sees two figures on their feet slowly pulling a third person from the truck. His mind whirls, 'this was not part of the plan?' For some strange reason he admonishes himself for stating the obvious. The ocean rollers make a loud noise but, even so, he slows his walk as if to remain undetected. He realises he is shaking. With no logical reasoning he now holds the gun out unsteadily in front of himself. As he gets to some 25 yards from what are now three people standing Sly Snake looks along the beach and wipes blood from his eyes. He blinks and stares at James. James stops in his tracks. As James is frozen Sly turns and taps King Snake on the shoulder. King slowly turns and his stare hardens on James. James blinks as he seems to see the skin behind King Snakes neck expand. A voice in his head screams 'oh fuck oh fuck oh fuck!' He sees King Snake speak to Sly and Si now. They immediately separate so to be standing 3 or 4 yards from each other. James notices they are all limping badly. He doesn't know which one to point the gun at; he settles for King Snake. Suddenly he hears King Snake's deep voice,

'Where is the Woodpecker?'

James wonders if he is hearing correctly. 'Woodpecker'? 'Woodpecker'? What the fuck is he on about?'

Sly and Si are scanning the objects that were in the SnakeTruck but are now strewn over the beach. James tries to work out which one to shoot first but his mind is frozen. His consciousness begins too sink. His mind swims in random thoughts. In the midst of this

his eye is taken by a movement at the upturned truck. A long dark shadow begins to emerge from the rear of the truck. Time freezes, his mind freezes and the gun in his hand seems to double in weight. He tries to point the gun at the shadow. He hears Sly Snake shout, 'Snakedog!' The shadow suddenly swivels from on its back and James realises it is some kind of dog. He is now convinced this is a nightmare. He can't wake. Snakedog is long and low slung. Some crazy muscular daschund. its black coat shines in the moonlight. He hears a voice shout 'Snakedog Kill.' He sees the dog look around until it sees him. It then rapidly accelerates towards him. The dogs white teeth clearly visible as it emits a strange growl. Whatever, it triggers some kind of wakeup call in James' mind. Some remnant of Doctor Charlie's medication kicks into gear. James points the pistol at the advancing dog. He fires once and the dog keeps coming. He fires again with the same result. He whimpers as he fires a third time with the Snakedog about 10 yards away. The bullet finds a mark on the animal's back. It howls and falls. It rolls and now it seems its rear legs are paralysed. It truly slithers like a snake now screaming at James. As it gets closer James finds the presence of mind to wait until he can't miss. He fires a 4th time and Snakedog is quiet and still with a bullet through its head. It is frozen motionless in the soft sand.

King Snake is now limping slowly towards James. His 'hood' massively visible. Sly Snake is also approaching having found a large hunting knife amongst the debris. Si Snake is still looking around amongst the items. James points the gun and tells them to 'freeze.' He hears his own voice sounding ridiculous and having no effect on either King or Sly. Instead he freezes himself.

The sound of the ocean seems to change its timbre now, for no reason. So much so, everyone stops. The noise gets louder and James realises it is an engine. He swivels to look behind himself as one, two and then three Harleys swing around from the ramp down to the hard sand lower down the beach. Each of the riders produce sawn offs from somewhere on the bike and before James can think they are past him. Three blasts in quick succession shock his sensitive musician's ears. Sly Snake flies backwards and hits the sand. Si Snake shortly afterwards. King is hit and staggers to his knees before falling onto his back. James sinks to his knees in shock.

The bikes sweep around on the hard sand and move towards him. They stop their engines and Don, Marv and Al step off. Al and Marv check on the fallen bodies. Don stands over King Snake and a fourth blast makes his body jump. James sinks further to the ground as King Snake seems to make one final effort to levitate himself. One last long gurgle-hiss before he lies motionless on the sand.

Last Pistol Shot

James slowly tilts forward until his elbows hit the sand. He grips Lucy's pistol still. His breathing quick and shallow.

Marv walks over to him and helps him to his feet.

'Well you certainly got some balls Jimmy E!', he pauses before continuing, 'You'd never make an angel. But, you do got balls.'

Don laughs, 'In your case we are guardian angels!'

Angel Al has been wandering around the beach looking at the detritus. He walks over with a strange boxy looking weapon. Don is immediately alerted to it,

'Al! You be careful with that thing.'

Al points it to the sand and pulls the trigger. It begins to jump in his hand sounding like a woodpecker. James then realises what King Snake had meant when he was asking where the woodpecker was. Al manages to control the gun and Don walks over and takes it.

A slight movement from the upturned SnakeTruck alerts them now as AJ Snake's head emerges and she slowly crawls out of the rear of the truck. Blood pours down the side of her face from a head wound. Her straight black hair reflects the clear moonlight. They watch her struggle to her feet. James automatically walks over to help her. She looks at him in dazed surprise. As she looks around she sees the bodies of the two dead Snake Brothers. She looks down impassively. Don pumps his Winchester to put a cartridge into the breach. James supports AJ as she stumbles towards the body of King Snake. She looks down at him for a few seconds before spitting on his face. Marv flinches. Don is first to break the silence,

'She's got to go?', he looks at Marv as if seeking confirmation.

James immediately stands in front of her, 'No! Enough madness.'

Marv laughs, 'Jimmy English! Always chasing pussy. You're a bad person.'

Angel Al begins to raise his weapon still working to Don's last instruction. There is what seems as first like a gust of wind. A sound like paper blowing in the breeze. Enough to make them turn their heads. A shadow passes across the moon and Al is suddenly enveloped by the large feathered bird. He shouts and struggles but loses the battle and finishes flat on his back on the sand. The eagle flies off with Al's Winchester pump gun in its talons. It soars into the sky and then out over the bay. From about 100 metres height and clearly visible in moonlight reflecting off the ocean it drops the shotgun into the middle of the bay. Al stands up indignant and embarrassed, 'Goddam fuckin ducks!'

AJ turns to face Don. She looks straight into his eyes as she uses her hands to move the curtain of hair away from the blooded side of her face. James looks at the wound. He takes his handkerchief out and dabs at the wound. AJ grabs the material herself and holds it to the wound.

'I'll live!'

She stares at Don, selecting him as the leader, before continuing.

'They're gone. I'm glad.'

She pauses again.

'I am my mother's daughter and that (she points at King) was never my father nor them (she gesticulates towards Sly and Si) my brothers. They have owned my mother and I for as long as I can remember. I am Ajei and my mother is Ooljee. We have sought freedom for years now. My mother has paid with her youth and beauty.'

She staggers. James quickly helps her. Don still stares holding his weapon.

Ajei makes a kind of yodelling sound now. Part music and part wail. There's a fluttering sound from above and, again, a shadow crosses the moon. The large eagle lands on the upturned Snake-Truck and stares at Don. He doesn't react. Ajei continues,

'White man want the money?'

She staggers to the rear of the SnakeTruck and retrieves a metal suitcase. She throws it onto the ground in front of Don. A quick blast from his Winchester blows the padlock away. Don opens the case to reveal banded sheaves of high denominations. They stare. Ajei continues, 'White man powder also.'

She retrieves a second case and drops it next to the first one. Don opens this to reveal it packed with bags of white powder.

Marv and Don load the drugs into their panier bags pausing only to throw one bag onto the floor around the bodies. They leave the opened case between the bodies too. They split the cash taking 10 or so sheaves and leaving the rest in the case.

Marv looks at Don and Al.

'Time we weren't here. The rest is yours Jimmy E. Time to get outta here!'

Don uncocks his Winchester and they move to their Harleys. They holster their weapons and ride off along the beach, up the ramp and away into the night.

James looks at Ajei. She speaks in dialect to the eagle. She moves around the back of the SnakeTruck and retrieves her bass guitar in its hard case and a rucksack. The eagle looks intently in the direction of the moon and out to sea. James turns to look too and sees the blood from three bodies carried in rivulets where small streams they are lain on flow to the sea. Under the moonlight it looks like snakes slithering into the sea. Ajei speaks to the eagle once again and it soars away.

James supports Ajei up the path to The Dog. He puts the case of remaining cash on the seat between them and they drive off. They drive in silence other than James shivering and coughing now. At one point Ajei retrieves a small pouch from her rucksack. She wets a finger in her mouth and then dips it into the pouch. She paints the dark powder on her tongue. She waits a few seconds before sighing in some sign of contentment. She then looks at James with concern. She licks her finger again and dips it into the pouch. This time she leans over and puts her finger to his lips. He opens his mouth and she slides her finger slowly in and along his tongue. He licks and swallows. As the urban streetlights now pass he feels some strength return.

As they hit town the sun is rising. There is no conversation with Ajei. James drives through the quiet city streets now as he tries to remember the way to Folsom Street Bus Station. Ajei gazes from the windows of The Dog transfixed by the city. The watered low morning sun catches her raven black cropped hair. It seems to act like some kind of black body radiator. It accepts all light falling on it and then emits subtle spectra depending on the tilt of her head. James sneaks more and more glances at her. Eventually he parks on

Beale Street opposite the Greyhound Bus Station. He turns to look at Ajei. He finds it difficult to speak but eventually,

'Sorry for the way things went down.'

She slowly turns and fixes his gaze. Her face looks different as she has stopped the headwound bleeding and cleaned much of the blood. She looks at the cityscape around her.

'White settlers have changed it all.'

James looks away. Hiding his desperate need to look at her more. He opens the case between them and she looks at the money. She looks back at James. She takes six wedges of high denominations. She also takes a few loose hundred dollar bills from the case. She stares at James looking deep into his eyes. He can't look away. Eventually Ajei's eyes slowly close. James' eyes remain open. He is transfixed now. Marv was right! Her eyes open and she gives him the leather pouch full of black powder. She slowly slides her finger into her mouth to remind him. He wonders if she is torturing him. She takes a hooded sweatshirt from her rucksack and slips it on over the black/grey snakeskin jacket she is still wearing from the gig. She speaks,

'Many bad people in this world. Less today than yesterday.'

She opens the door and athletically steps down to the street. Her graceful movements returned. She reaches behind the seat and retrieves her bass guitar. Now James aches for her to stay. She looks at him one last time and walks across Beale Street and into the bus station.

***

The Dog is parked at the top of Taylor Street next to Ina Coolbrith Park. James and Lucy look at the bay in the distance. Lucy in a hoodie and hiding her face. James had picked her up from the flat while still early and just driven at random and here they end up.

James smiles at her, 'No need for the hoodie look now Mrs Lucy Smith!'

As she turns to him he sees a smile he's never seen before. Maybe behind her eyes? Maybe he is beginning to see what Ajei sees. Maybe it's the powder she gave him that he uses now.

'Where you gonna go Mr Jimmy Smith?'

'Figured I'd go north.'

She holds his hand. Highway 101 runs through her mind.

'You take care.'

'Hardly necessary now.'

'Apart from the fact that you will have lawmen and bounty hunters on your trail.'

'You are attracted to bad people like me Lucy Smith!'

She laughs, 'Not now I'm a married woman! You're just a soft hearted limey Jimmy Smith – AND – and full of shit!'

James unexpectedly breaks down in tears.

Lucy looks at him in silence as he regains his composure.

He asks, 'All that's left of us is love?'

'Still making up songs Jimmy Smith? You and Morrissey are my favourite Englishmen.'

'Well that one is Philip Larkin.'

'Who's he?'

'The greatest.'

He smiles as a beam of sunlight now illuminates The Dog.

'I got to go now Lucy Smith. You got that money?'

She nods, 'Yes, it's a lot.'

She pats her duffel bag. She steps out of The Dog and walks around it for one last look. He steps onto the sidewalk beside her. She pats The Dog's hood. She turns to James,

'Never in the history of transportation has so much been owed to … an old shitbox truck!'

They laugh until James speaks,

'Remember me to Nick Lucas Lucy.'

'Sure.'

'No long goodbyes for this boy – but will you do something for me?'

'Sure?'

'Look after our little girl?'

'How'd you know it's a girl?'

'I know!'

James moves towards the Dog Truck. She holds his hands. She wishes for Boris The Cranium's time machine.

'I mean it Lucy Smith – no long goodbyes for me.'

Lucy is dazed. James climbs into the truck seat. He winds the window down.

'My Mum is called Joan. And is no bad person.' He drives off.

Lucy walks into the park and sits. She stares at the sunrise. Shadows and dark clouds begin to clear from her mind. She thinks of James, she thinks of her Mum, she thinks of her Dad. Her tears run like a clear mountain stream now.

James drives across town once more. He walks into the Dirtkickers HQ. Thunderman and The Gnome stare at him. Mike Remo appears from the back room. They look at each other in silence. TMan breaks it,

'Marv called by.'

James nods.

Of all people, Mike Remo breaks down and sinks to his knees. In 5 years James has seen him handle anything an audience could (literally or otherwise) throw at him. It shocks James to see him like this. James walks over and sinks to his knees embracing Mike. The other two Dirtkickers join them.

As James makes his way to the door now he gives Mike a cassette tape, 'Here's some songs.'

At the door he turns, 'You need a new guitar player, why not try Lucy?'

James walks quickly out and fires up The Dog. The three Dirtkickers are now stood at the door. James winds down the window and smiles. He gives the skulk rock salute and shouts out the skulk rock mantra,

'KEEP ON FUCKIN ROCKIN!'

They laugh through tears. 'Keep on fuckin rockin limey bastard.'

***

He drives The Dog over The Golden Gate heading north. The scenery of Highway 101 unfolds in front of The Dog one more time. As evening falls he makes Crescent City. He finds a Hotel on Main Street with a window overlooking various revelry bars. The receptionist looks at him suspiciously as he pays cash in advance with a large denomination bill and tells her no change is necessary.

In his room, he looks in the mirror and is shocked by his appearance now. No wonder the receptionist looked suspicious. His breathing shallow and desperate now. He resorts to Dr Charlie's stronger medicine and two fingers of Ajei's black powder. The joint medication beats back the evil.

He phones his Mum in England. She's so so happy to hear from him. She tells him how she is so busy and has lots of friends. She goes for coffee with her friends 3 times a week. She has trips to the cinema. She helps with the local amateur dramatic society. She tells him that cousin Jill is finally getting married to a guy from Oldham. He's got a good job in sales although she doesn't quite know what he sells. Aunt Clara has bought at least 4 Mother Of The Bride dresses because she can't decide which one suits her best.

Details that would have driven him mad with boredom now seem so so important to him. Eventually the conversation has to end. He tells his mother how much he loves her and how he thinks of her everyday.

He puts the phone down and smiles. He thinks of her smiling face.

He is calm now as he reaches into his rucksack and takes out Lucy's pistol. There is one cartridge, of the five it held, still left in there. He shudders as he remembers firing the other four at the SnakeDog. He clears his mind of those thoughts. He thinks of some of his songs. He thinks of Lucy Smith. He thinks of Felicia. He thinks of Mike Remo. He thinks of Thunderman. He thinks of The Gnome and his strange dance. He thinks of Ajei, He thinks of his Mum. He thinks of his Dad. He thinks of Bob Dylan. He thinks of Gabriella Sabatini. He thinks of Stevie Nicks and Chrissie Hynde. He thinks of Dr Charlie. He thinks of Lucy. He thinks of Little Joan. He thinks of Lucy again. He imagines what little Joan will be like? He thinks of Felicia. Again, he thinks of Mike Remo, TMan and The Gnome. He gives the Skulk Rock salute. His other hand feels the cruel stainless steel of the pistol.

On the street below, revellers gather undercover outside a rowdy bar as a clear moon is visible between big heartless rainbearing clouds. The summer is gone.

Last Pistol Shot

https://badpeoplethemusical.bandcamp.com/track/last-pistol-shot

The rain beats on a hotel window pane
And laughter in the street below

Life goes on like a hurricane
But for me it moves so slow

One more dream and one more pill
I'm thinking back – what I had and what I got
The clock ticks but time stands still
I'm looking down the barrel
Of my last pistol shot

I wish that the stars would turn around
My dreams are all twisted
My gravity is sinking down
And time is telling me that I never existed

The world is turning still
I'm looking at your picture and I still like it a lot
I'm still here but I'm still ill
I'm looking down the barrel
Of my last pistol shot

Well nothing ever comes back
It's a one way track
A one way ticket on a fast train express
Tterminating next stop and that is that

So pass me a pencil
As you pass the pistol
I need to get a message
To anyone who cares to listen

The world don't owe me a thing
I won and I wasted a lot
I'm not crying and I'm not complaining
I'm looking down the barrel
Of my last pistol shot

None of the revellers below hear the dull boom of the pistol. None
of the revellers notice the flash of light from the 2nd floor room.

*

Life goes on.

Starkeepers

A wooded glade with shafts of sunlight streaming down. A figure sits on a log. An older man walks through the woods and into the glade; he approaches the sitting figure from the rear. The sitting figure is gazing down at his hands and not moving. The older man stands behind him in silence for a while before speaking softly.

'James?'

The sitting figure IS James and he turns in surprise and amazement, 'Dad?'

'Well I'm a 'Starkeeper' now!', his father beams.

James looks shocked. The Starkeeper continues, 'I know it's a surprise. I had a similar surprise.'

'Am I dreaming?'

'Nope. You're what we call a 'waiter'.'

'What the fuck?'

'LANGUAGE James!', The Starkeeper admonishes before continuing. 'It has been deemed necessary that your situation is to be considered further before your full admission to the starlife.'

'Hey Dad, don't bullshit me?'

'Golly James you even talk like an American these days!'

James stares at his father for an extended period before his tears arrive and before rushing forward to embrace him.

'Dad, I'm sorry!'

'I'm sorry I was single minded about your future. And sorry I didn't appreciate your music. And sorry I was too protective.'

They smile in silence. James speaks first, 'So. After all the bollocks religions on earth it turns out that the universe runs like the gospel according to Rodgers and Hammerstein?'

'Bluntly put James but, nonetheless – ACCURATE!'

'It always was your favourite eh?'

'Well, yes it was!', The Starkeeper breaks into song (badly), 'When you walk through a storm … Hold your head up high … ', he does a little dance and smiles, 'You see you got your skulk rock talent from me 'Jimmy E'!'

They laugh. Mr Smith suddenly turns serious, 'The thing is James you have been a 'Bad Person'!', he wags his finger and continues, 'THE Powers that be decided you can be a 'waiter' and if you prove yourself diligent then they will reconsider your situation.'

'What the fuck does that mean?'

'For a start it means you can mend your potty mouth young man!'

'Sorry!'

'And the rest of the time you are to watch out for your friend Lucy. And of course for Little Joan.'

James looks confused but then asks tentatively, 'Little Joan is my daughter?'

'Yes James and you are to stand guard until she comes of age!'

'Yes of course!'

'She is three and a half now. Your case has been a tricky one!'

'When can I see her?'

'I will take you there now but your task will be to keep 'The Night Shadows' at bay.'

'The Night Shadows?'

'Yes, they bring a variety of evil to the world.'

'How do I spot them? And, how do I protect her?'

Starkeeper gives him a small box.

'This will show their approach. You'll get the hang of it – and your love will protect her.'

He gives James the box before continuing, 'You will be able to fly and look around the old earth but you must be diligent and vigilant – remember James – 'All that's left of us is love'!'

'So Philip Larkin was right? As well as Rodgers and Hammerstein?'

'Yes, indeed!'

'Will you help me Dad?'

'I would love to but I am looking out for your mother at the moment!'

'Is she ok?'

'She is older James and misses you so terribly!'

'So sorry Dad!', James breaks down.

His father The Starkeeper comforts him before explaining, 'Come on I'll show you where they are! One day we will all be together!'

They both smile.

***

San Francisco sits in early morning sun. its light streams into a high bedroom window in a house at the top of a hill. 'James' sits on the apex of the roof above. Inside the room a gorgeous little girl wakes up. Lucy Smith comes into her room smiling, 'What should we do today Little Joan?'

Joan smiles as she thinks, 'Painting!'

Lucy laughs, 'Ok but should we go see the seals first?'

'Yes!', Little Joan smiles and leaps out of her bed.

Next, we see James smiles as he watches Lucy and Joan leave the house.

He hovers as he accompanies them skipping down the hill.

At the piers Joan meets a little friend and they smile and hug.

We see the children running on the Pier and barking at the seals. The mothers all chat.

James soars and swoops over the scene.

As the day wears on we see Joan and Lucy painting in the flat.

As night falls we see Joan going to bed and James sat on the same roof bay looking at his starkeeper warning box for any stray snakes of evil.

He misses his last life. He wishes he was down there making up songs. He still makes up songs but there's no way he can send them (although he often stands close to Lucy and tries to send her songs when she opens her notebook). He looks at the traffic continually flowing over the Bay Bridge. He wonders about The Dog. He worries about the pollution. He worries about the world of men. He worries about all these things because of Little Joan.

He still makes up songs.

He worries about Skulk Rock.

The Floating Ghost

https://badpeoplethemusical.bandcamp.com/track/the-floating-ghost

I'm looking from a window and I can't see a tree
I'm in a desert city in the land of luxury
A woman in a fur coat is walkin' up the street
She got the light in her eyes but she can't see me

I am the floating ghost
That no-one ever knows
And I go places no-one ever goes

I arrive from the skies and I float away untouched
To the heart of the stars where all light is crushed
All the night time sounds – I conduct
I'm the genius that was always overlooked

Float over Mexico
Float over Idaho
I float anywhere I want to go

I am The Floating Ghost

I look down on this earth – from way up high
I don't understand – how I can fly
I got eyes so wide – there ain't no place to hide
You can lock your doors but I just float inside

I am the floating ghost
That no-one ever knows
And I go places no-one ever goes

Float in the summer heat
Float over Downing Street
I float in the places old ghosts meet

And I trail the Taliban
And I view the Vatican
And I piss in the Palace of Buckingham

Ghost Radar

It's evening and Lucy is reading Little Joan a story. Joan is entranced. Eventually Lucy says, 'c'mon Little Joan, it's time for bed.' Little Joan stalls for time and asks, as she always does,

'Can we see if the moon is out tonight Mom?'

Lucy carries Little Joan to the window because she always wants to see if the moon is there. That night it is. It looks so so close as it hovers over San Francisco Bay. James sits on the roof above and looks at the same moon.

Little Joan asks, 'Are there people on the moon Mummy?'

'Nobody knows for sure?'

'I can see them Mummy!'

'You better behave then Little Joan. They are watching you.'

Little Joan nods.

Lucy carries her over to bed. As she is tucked in she suddenly remembers what she always remembers, 'Mom, can we check the ghost radar?'

Lucy smiles and takes out her phone and boots up the Ghost Radar app. Little Joan asks, 'Is our ghost there?'

'Yes – there he is Joan, as always!'

They see a flashing light on the screen. Little Joan looks a little apprehensive, she asks, 'Mommy, it's not a scary ghost?'

'No Little Joan – only Bad People get scary ghosts!'

Little Joan smiles, 'We're not Bad People are we Mommy?'

Lucy smiles at her, 'No Little Joan YOU are not a bad person – AND – you seem to have a Guardian Angel!'

They stare at the Ghost Radar screen and the flashing light on screen marks a big cross-kiss onto the screen. They both blow it kisses.

Ghost Radar

https://badpeoplethemusical.bandcamp.com/track/ghost-radar

I got a phone with ghost radar
And man they are everywhere
There was one in the back of my car
When I was going somewhere

The darkness of the next world
Don't screen my sight
I'm on the 6th sense network
And my phone is fully charged tonight

Ghost Radar
I know where they are
There's 2 in my backyard
Switched on my ghost radar
Ghost Radar Ghost Radar

They don't need no tickets
They don't need no doors
They don't worry about traffic
And they don't need no cars

I heard it on the news today
A dead man got up and walked away
I'm sitting in a high window bay
As life and death – pass me by

If I'm lonely at night
Switch on my ghost radar
A ghostly light
Is never very far
Magnetic disturbances
talkin' to me … talkin to me..

Do you feel like you're never alone?
Do you hear footsteps following you home?
Maybe a dream you've always known
Maybe a mystery message on your mobile phone

Ghost Radar Ghost Radar
Ghost Radar Ghost Radar

Lists of Love

Lucy Smith is on stage with The Lowdown Dirtkickers. Mike Remo introduces her to the large crowd and says, 'Our guitar player and songwriter Lucy Smith is going to sing this one for you.'

As she moves to the mic Lucy speaks to the audience,

'You know – sometimes songs just appear from nowhere. It's like a ghost visits and gives them to you. All you have to do is write it down and sing it. This is one of those songs.'

(Pause)

'You know what they say? "All That's Left Of Us Is Love"? Well, make sure there's something left of you - and you will always stay in The Lists Of Love! This song is for JIMMY ENGLISH.'

The audience cheer.

She looks across and behind at Mike Remo, Thunderman and The Gnome. They smile and strike the Skulk Rock salute. The considerable audience does the Skulk Rock salute. The Lowdown Dirtkickers are top of The Skulk Rock Charts.

Lists of Love

{https://badpeoplethemusical.bandcamp.com/track/the-lists-of-love }

I want to stay in the lists of love
Be there when push comes to shove
I'm a heart angel from above
And you are what I'm thinking of

I'll summon all the magic shadows tonight
All the tracks and tricks of the light
You cut a heart shaped hole in my soul
So I can never die, never even get old
And if blood might fall on England's green
Sands of time from across the sea

This is evil that could come to be
But I mostly just think of you and me

No need for a pension plan
Might be old but I was once a man
This is not a heart that love deserts
This is not a love that comes in spurts
As I finally admit defeat
My ghost will sniff your sheets
My dark desires cannot be destroyed
I'm gonna be touching you across the void

Time took these eyes and made them blurred
A passing year is just a four letter word
But time turns round and time turns back
All my dreams are still intact
You are nailed to my memory
Crucified across my heart
Time has been and time has gone
Of all I've seen you are still the one

The audience of SkulkRockers cheer. They know the truths of this world as it carries on in all it's ignorant glory outside the venue.

***

PostScript:

Boris The Cranium has finally completed his unification theories. His mathematical ramblings show conclusively that there are parallel worlds to this one. Not many people believe him though. They prefer to cling to their beliefs in good versus evil and an 'afterlife' dependent upon the balance of each over a whole lifetime.

38105497R00122

Printed in Poland
by Amazon Fulfillment
Poland Sp. z o.o., Wrocław